AMINATA'S JOURNEY: A Tale of Strength and Survival

EDDIE INYANGALA

Published by EDDIE INYANGALA, 2024.

AMINATA'S JOURNEY: A TALE OF STRENGTH AND SURVIVAL

First edition. June 28, 2024.

Copyright © 2024 EDDIE INYANGALA.

ISBN: 979-8224361885

Written by EDDIE INYANGALA.

To the resilient spirit of all those who endured unimaginable hardships and yet found the strength to dream of freedom. This story is for the ancestors whose courage and unwavering hope light the path for future generations.

To my beloved family, for their endless support and inspiration, and to the readers, may you find in Aminata's journey a testament to the indomitable human spirit.

With deepest gratitude,

Eddie Inyangala

AMINATA'S
JOURNEY

A Tale of Strength and Survival

· · · ·

EDDIE INYANGALA

Independently published

DEDICATION

To the resilient spirit of all those who endured unimaginable hardships and yet found the strength to dream of freedom. This story is for the ancestors whose courage and unwavering hope light the path for future generations.
To my beloved family, for their endless support and inspiration, and to the readers, may you find in Aminata's journey a testament to the indomitable human spirit.
With deepest gratitude,
Eddie Inyangala

CONTENTS

ACKNOWLEDGMENTS

To the communities whose stories inspired Aminata's journey, thank you for your resilience and courage. This book is a tribute to your strength and endurance.

To my readers, thank you for opening your hearts to Aminata's story. Your willingness to embark on this journey with her means more than words can express.

With deepest gratitude,

Eddie Inyangala

1 The Heart of the Village

. . . .

AMINATA'S STORY BEGINS in a village named Moyu, a village wedged between two life-giving rivers, nestled deep within the lush, verdant landscapes of West Africa. This village, whose name translates to "the heart of the forest," was a sanctuary of natural beauty and rich traditions. The land was a mixture of vibrant greenery, towering trees, and fertile soil that provided bountiful harvests for the people living there.

At the center of the village stood a majestic tree, its thick, twisted trunk and sprawling branches a symbol of life, wisdom, and continuity. The tree was ancient, its roots intertwining with the history and stories of the village. It was under this sacred that Aminata entered the world, a new life beginning under the watchful gaze of the elders and the protective canopy of the tree.

. . . .

THE DAY OF AMINATA'S birth was a day of celebration. The sky was a clear, deep blue, the sun shining brightly but gently, as if blessing the new arrival. The villagers gathered around the baobab tree, their faces alight with anticipation and joy. The women sang songs of welcome and praise, their voices rising and falling in harmonious unison, a sound as old as the earth itself.

"Quick, quick! Cover Abeni well!" yelled Mama Zuri, her voice cutting through the air like a knife. The women hurried, forming a tight circle around Abeni, their colorful skirts and head-wraps fluttering in the breeze. They used large cloths and blankets to shield her from curious eyes, ensuring her privacy during the sacred moment.

"Oy! You men, scatter!" shouted Mama Zuri again, waving her hands dramatically. "No be your place dis one! Go chase goat or something!"

The men, some chuckling, some pretending to look offended, obediently turned away, retreating to a respectful distance. "Abeni strong woman," muttered one of the elders, his eyes twinkling with pride. "She give us another hunter, for sure."

The children, wide-eyed and curious, were gently but firmly herded away by their mothers. "Go on, go on," they were told, "no need to be seeing all dis now. Later you go hear the story, no worry."

Inside the circle, Abeni's face was a mask of concentration, her strong hands gripping the arms of the women beside her. She was surrounded by the warmth and support of her community, their songs filling the air, blending with the sounds of the forest and the river.

"E go be okay, Abeni," whispered Mama Zuri, her voice filled with reassurance. "We dey with you. Dis pikin go come fine, you go see."

And then, with one final, powerful push, Aminata entered the world. The cry of the newborn was met with a collective cheer from the women, their joy bursting forth like a dam breaking. Abeni, exhausted but triumphant, held her daughter high, presenting her to the sky and the spirits of their ancestors.

"Praise be to the gods!" she exclaimed, her voice strong despite her fatigue. "Dis na Aminata, our future, our joy!"

The women ululated, their voices carrying the sound of celebration through the village. The men, hearing the joyous noise, knew the birth had been successful and began to cheer as well, their voices adding to the cacophony of happiness.

"Ah, she strong like her papa!" shouted one of the men, raising his hands in salute.

Standing beside Abeni was Ade, Aminata's father. Ade was the village's best hunter, a man revered for his skill, bravery, and wisdom. His tall, muscular frame and confident demeanor spoke of countless successful hunts and adventures. Yet, at this moment, his strength seemed to soften, his heart swelling with a profound joy as he gazed upon his firstborn child.

However, when he saw that the baby was a girl, his smile faltered just a bit. "Ah, I dey hope for small hunter, but...," he began, scratching his head. But as he looked into Aminata's eyes, his heart melted completely. "But, dis one go be great too," he finished with a grin, his initial disappointment fading away.

"Abeni, you do well," he whispered, his eyes never leaving his wife and newborn daughter. He silently vowed to protect and nurture her with all his might, even if she wasn't the little hunter he had initially hoped for.

The women, overhearing his comment, burst into laughter. "Ade, you go see, dis pikin go hunt hearts, not animals!" one of them teased, making everyone around them laugh even louder.

"True, true," another woman chimed in, "She go make you proud, Ade, you go see."

Ade joined in the laughter, his heart full of joy and pride. Despite his fleeting disappointment, he was overwhelmed with love for his daughter. The sight of Aminata, so small and perfect, brought tears to his eyes.

As the villagers celebrated, the women began to clean up, still chattering excitedly. "You see how she dey hold am up? Strong woman, dat one," said one of the younger women, her eyes shining with admiration.

"Abi," agreed another, "dis pikin go grow sabi plenty tings. She go be great."

And so, under the protective canopy of the ancient baobab tree, Aminata's life began. Her arrival was marked by love, joy, and the unwavering support of her community, a beginning as bright and promising as the clear blue sky above.

....

FROM THE MOMENT AMINATA was born, her parents took great care to protect her from any harm, physical or spiritual. On the seventh day after her birth, a naming ceremony had been held. Ade, holding his tiny daughter, had whispered her name three times into her ear, ensuring that the spirits recognized and protected her.

The elders of the village had gathered, their faces serious and their voices low, as they performed rituals to ward off evil spirits. "Dis pikin must be protected from witches," one of the elders had muttered, her eyes scanning the surrounding forest. The villagers believed strongly in the power of witches to bring harm, and newborns were especially vulnerable.

To safeguard Aminata, Abeni had tied a small leather amulet around her waist. "Dis go keep bad spirits away," she had explained, her voice soothing. The amulet, filled with herbs and blessed by the village shaman, was a powerful talisman against evil.

Despite the protective measures, Aminata's early years were not without challenges. When she was just a toddler, she fell ill with a fever that left her weak and listless. Her parents were frantic with worry, fearing the worst.

"Ade, go fetch Baba Olu," Abeni urged, her voice trembling. Baba Olu was the village healer, a man renowned for his knowledge of herbs and healing rituals. Ade ran through the village, his heart pounding with fear and determination.

When Baba Olu arrived, he examined Aminata carefully, his hands gentle but firm. "Dis fever strong, but we go fight it," he said, his voice calm and reassuring. He prepared a concoction of herbs, grinding them into a paste and mixing it with water. "She go drink dis, and we go pray to the gods for her healing."

For days, Baba Olu stayed with Aminata, administering his herbal remedies and chanting prayers. Slowly, the fever broke, and Aminata's strength returned. Her parents wept with relief, thanking Baba Olu and the gods for her recovery.

Aminata's early years were a tapestry of laughter, learning, and discovery. From the moment she could walk, she was a bundle of energy and curiosity, eager to explore the world around her. The village was her playground, and the natural world her classroom. She spent her days running through the tall grasses, their tips brushing against her legs as she chased butterflies and imagined herself as a great explorer.

The sturdy trees became her companions and teachers. She learned to climb their branches with agility and confidence, each ascent a new adventure. From her perch high above the ground, she could see the village spread out below her, a patchwork of thatched roofs and winding paths. The river, a shimmering ribbon of blue, flowed gently beyond, its waters a source of sustenance and joy.

Swimming in the cool, clear waters of the river was one of Aminata's favorite activities. She delighted in the feeling of the water against her skin, the gentle current carrying her along. She would dive beneath the surface, her eyes wide open, exploring the underwater world of fish and plants. The river was her friend, its ever-changing flow a constant source of wonder and excitement.

. . . .

AS SHE GREW OLDER, Aminata's bold spirit became evident. She was fearless, often leading the village children in games and adventures. Her confidence and energy made her a natural leader, but it also led to conflicts. Aminata had a habit of bullying the other children, pushing them around and insisting on getting her way.

"Why you dey always do like dat?" her friend Duni asked one day, rubbing his arm where Aminata had pushed him. "You no fit play nice?"

Aminata, her eyes flashing, shrugged. "I be de leader. Dem for follow me."

But the other children grew tired of her bossiness. One day, after yet another quarrel, they decided to fight back. When Aminata tried to push Duni again, he and the others stood their ground. A scuffle ensued, and Aminata, taken aback by their resistance, ended up with a bloody nose and a bruised ego.

Aminata ran home, tears streaming down her face. "Mama, dem hit me!" she wailed, clutching her aching nose.

Abeni, ever the wise and patient mother, gently cleaned her daughter's wounds. "Aminata, you strong, but you no fit bully others," she said softly. "You must learn to lead with kindness, not force."

Ade, overhearing the conversation, nodded in agreement. "You sabi how to be strong, but strength no mean say you for push people around. You for protect, guide, and help dem."

Aminata, her tears drying, listened to her parents' words. She realized they were right. Being a leader was not just about being strong, but about being fair and kind. It was a lesson she took to heart, one that would shape her character in the years to come.

Despite these early challenges, Aminata's childhood was filled with joy and discovery. She continued to explore the world around her, her curiosity and energy undiminished. She forged strong bonds with her friends, learning the importance of loyalty and respect.

Her parents remained her greatest protectors and teachers. Ade taught her the skills of hunting and tracking, while Abeni shared the art of storytelling and the wisdom of their ancestors. Under their guidance, Aminata grew into a strong, intelligent, and compassionate young girl.

Her early years were a mix of laughter, lessons, and love, setting the foundation for the remarkable journey that lay ahead. Aminata's spirit, shaped by her experiences and the people who loved her, was ready to face whatever challenges the future might hold.

4 Lessons from a Father

. . . .

AMINATA'S FATHER, ADE, took great pride in teaching his daughter the ways of the forest. He was a patient and attentive teacher, his deep voice filled with knowledge and love. He taught her how to track animals, showing her the subtle signs that most would overlook. Broken twigs, a patch of disturbed earth, the faintest hint of a scent in the air—all were clues that told a story to those who knew how to read them.

Under Ade's guidance, Aminata learned to understand the whispers of the forest. She discovered how to listen to the sounds of the trees, the rustling of leaves, and the calls of the animals. The forest was alive with messages, and Ade taught her how to interpret them, how to sense the presence of a deer or the approach of a storm.

Respecting the balance of nature was a lesson Ade emphasized above all else. He taught Aminata that every creature, no matter how small, played a vital role in the ecosystem. The forest was a delicate web of life, and it was their duty to protect and preserve it. Ade's teachings instilled in Aminata a deep respect for nature, a reverence that would stay with her throughout her life.

. . . .

ONE SUNNY AFTERNOON, Ade decided to take Aminata deeper into the forest than they had ever gone before. "Aminata," he called, his voice booming across their compound, "we dey go far today. Make sure you sabi your steps well."

Aminata, ever eager for an adventure, quickly gathered her things. "Papa, I be ready! Make we go!"

They trekked through the dense forest, Ade pointing out various signs along the way. "You see dat broken branch?" he asked, crouching low. "Na sign say antelope don pass here."

Aminata nodded, her eyes wide with excitement. "I dey see, Papa. I go remember."

As they ventured further, the forest grew thicker and darker. Suddenly, Ade stopped, his hand shooting out to halt Aminata. "Quiet," he whispered. "You hear dat?"

Aminata strained her ears, but all she could hear was the rustling of leaves and distant bird calls. "I no hear anything, Papa."

Ade's eyes narrowed, his senses on high alert. "Stay close to me," he ordered, his voice low and serious.

Just as they took another step forward, a large, snarling animal leaped out from the underbrush. It was a wild boar, its eyes glowing with anger. Aminata froze, her heart pounding in her chest.

"Papa!" she screamed, stumbling backward.

Ade reacted quickly, pulling out his hunting spear. "Aminata, climb dat tree now!" he shouted, pointing to a nearby tree with low-hanging branches.

Aminata scrambled up the tree, her small hands gripping the rough bark. She watched in horror as her father faced the boar. The beast charged at Ade, who stood his ground, his spear ready.

The boar lunged, but Ade sidestepped, thrusting his spear into its side. The boar let out a blood-curdling scream, thrashing wildly. Ade held his ground, keeping his spear firm. Finally, with one last effort, the boar collapsed, its fierce eyes dimming.

Ade panted heavily, his muscles tense and his face grim. "Aminata, you dey okay?" he called up to her.

Aminata, still clinging to the tree, nodded shakily. "Yes, Papa. I dey okay."

Ade sighed with relief, wiping sweat from his brow. "Good. Make you come down now."

Aminata climbed down, her legs trembling. "Papa, you save me!" she exclaimed, throwing her arms around him.

Ade chuckled, patting her back. "I tell you say forest no be joke. You for always dey alert."

Aminata looked at the fallen boar, her eyes wide. "But Papa, I no sabi say boar fit be so dangerous."

Ade nodded, his expression serious. "Yes, Aminata. Dis na lesson for you. Forest get plenty secrets, and e no go always be kind. But if you sabi respect am, e go respect you back."

As they made their way back to the village, Aminata couldn't shake the fear she had felt. Her heart still pounded in her chest, and her legs felt weak. But she also felt a deep sense of admiration for her father, whose bravery had saved her.

The encounter with the boar left Aminata with a small scar on her arm, a reminder of that fateful day. She wore it with pride, a badge of her adventure and her father's heroism. Whenever the other children asked about it, she would recount the story with great enthusiasm, her eyes sparkling with excitement.

"You no go believe wetin happen dat day!" she would begin, her voice full of drama. "Papa and me dey forest when dis big, big boar jump out! I nearly faint, but Papa dey brave. He fight am and save me!"

The children listened in awe, their mouths agape. "Aminata, you dey lucky say your papa strong," one of them would say.

Aminata would nod, a mischievous grin on her face. "True, but I go strong too. I go learn everything Papa sabi."

Her parents watched with amusement and pride as Aminata regaled her friends with tales of bravery. Ade would often shake his head, a smile tugging at his lips. "Dis girl go be something else," he would say to Abeni. "She get fire for her belly."

Abeni would laugh, her eyes twinkling. "She be your daughter, Ade. She no go ever back down from challenge."

And so, Aminata's early years were filled with lessons from the forest and from her father. She learned to respect nature, to face her fears, and to never give up. Her adventures, though sometimes dangerous, shaped her into a strong and courageous young girl, ready to take on whatever challenges life would throw her way.

5 The Art of Storytelling

· · · ·

AMINATA'S MOTHER, ABENI, was the village's storyteller, a revered keeper of history and tradition. In the evenings, as the sun dipped below the horizon and the sky was painted with hues of orange and pink, the villagers would gather around the fire. It was during these magical moments that Abeni would weave her tales, her voice a melody that captivated all who listened.

Abeni's stories were a blend of history, myth, and morality, each one a treasure trove of lessons and entertainment. She spoke of the gods and spirits that watched over them, of brave ancestors who had faced incredible challenges, and of the animals that shared their world. Her tales were rich with vivid imagery and emotion, transporting her listeners to distant lands and forgotten times.

Aminata was entranced by her mother's storytelling. She would sit close to the fire, her eyes wide and her heart racing with excitement. She absorbed every word, every inflection, her imagination igniting with the possibilities of the stories. Over time, Abeni began to teach Aminata the art of storytelling, passing down the secrets and techniques that had been handed down through generations.

· · · ·

ONE OF AMINATA'S FAVORITE stories that her mother told was the legend of the Ogre of the Dark Forest. Abeni would spin a tale of a fearsome creature with glowing red eyes and sharp, gnashing teeth, which lurked in the shadows, waiting to devour unsuspecting travelers.

As Abeni recounted the tale, her voice would drop to a low, ominous whisper, sending shivers down the spines of her audience. The children huddled closer together, their eyes wide with fear and wonder, as they listened to her every word.

But amidst the fear, there was also laughter. One evening, as Abeni reached the climax of the story, describing the Ogre's bone-chilling roar, one of the younger children, overcome with terror, let out a squeal and promptly wet himself.

The other children erupted into giggles, their fear momentarily forgotten in the hilarity of the moment. Abeni paused in her storytelling, her eyes twinkling with amusement, before continuing with even greater gusto.

Despite the occasional mishap, Abeni's storytelling sessions were always a highlight of village life. She had a talent for captivating her audience, drawing them into her tales with her expressive gestures and melodious voice.

But Abeni's stories were more than just entertainment; they were also lessons in courage, kindness, and resilience. Through her words, she instilled in her listeners a sense of wonder and awe, inspiring them to face their own challenges with bravery and determination.

As Aminata grew older, she began to assist her mother in storytelling, taking on smaller roles and eventually crafting her own tales. Together, mother and daughter continued the tradition of storytelling, ensuring that the rich tapestry of their village's history and culture would be passed down to future generations.

And so, under the flickering light of the fire and the watchful gaze of the stars, Abeni and Aminata wove their stories, their voices blending with the crackle of the flames and the rustle of the evening breeze. It was a legacy of love and storytelling, a bond that would endure for generations to come.

• • • •

DESPITE HER STRENGTH, Abeni always showed respect and admiration for her husband, Ade. Even when he was angry or frustrated, she remained calm and composed, never speaking out of turn or questioning his authority.

One evening, after a particularly long and unsuccessful hunting expedition, Ade returned home in a foul mood. His temper flared at the slightest provocation, and Abeni knew to tread carefully around him.

As she prepared their evening meal, Abeni could sense the tension in the air. She moved quickly and quietly, hoping to avoid any conflict. But when she took a little longer than usual to bring Ade his food, he exploded with anger.

"Abeni, where is my food?!" he roared, his voice echoing through the house.

Abeni flinched, her heart pounding with fear. She hurried to the kitchen, her hands trembling as she plated the food. But before she could bring it to the table, Ade stormed into the kitchen, his face contorted with rage.

"Are you deaf, woman? I said, where is my food?!" he bellowed, his hand raised threateningly.

Aminata, watching from the doorway, felt a knot form in her stomach. She had never seen her father so angry, and she was scared.

But Abeni remained calm, her eyes steady as she met her husband's gaze. "I dey sorry, Ade. E go soon be ready," she said quietly, her voice barely above a whisper.

Ade's anger seemed to dissipate as quickly as it had come. He sighed heavily, his shoulders slumping with exhaustion. "I dey sorry too,

Abeni. E no be easy time for me," he murmured, his voice tinged with regret.

Abeni nodded, her expression softening. "I know, Ade. I dey understand."

And just like that, the tension in the room evaporated, replaced by an unspoken understanding between husband and wife.

After Ade had calmed down, Abeni and Aminata exchanged a glance, their eyes twinkling with mischief. "Mama, you see how Papa dey vex like ogre for forest?" Aminata whispered, barely able to contain her laughter.

Abeni chuckled, shaking her head. "Yes, my dear. Sometimes your papa fit be like ogre, but e get heart of gold."

Aminata giggled, the tension of the moment forgotten. "True, Mama. But if Papa dey ogre, you be lioness wey dey tame am!"

And with that, mother and daughter burst into laughter, their bond stronger than ever in the face of adversity. For Abeni and Aminata, humor was a powerful tool, capable of turning even the darkest moments into moments of light and laughter.

The bond between Aminata, Abeni, and Ade was unbreakable. They were a close-knit family, bound together by love, respect, and shared experiences. They spent countless hours together, whether it was tending to their garden, preparing meals, or simply enjoying each other's company. Their home was filled with laughter, stories, and the comforting presence of family.

Aminata cherished the moments she spent with her parents. She loved listening to her father's hunting tales, his voice full of excitement and pride. She adored her mother's gentle wisdom and the way she could turn even the simplest event into a captivating story. Together, they created a world of love and security, a foundation that would support Aminata throughout her life.

· · · ·

ONE OF AMINATA'S FAVORITE pastimes was listening to her father's hunting tales. Ade would regale her with stories of his adventures in the forest, each one more exciting than the last.

One particular story that Aminata loved to hear was the tale of the forgetful warthog. According to Ade, he and his fellow hunters had been lying in wait for hours, hidden among the bushes, waiting for the perfect moment to strike.

"Just as we were about to ambush the warthog," Ade would recount, his eyes gleaming with mischief, "it suddenly remembered it left its lunch behind and dashed in our direction!"

Aminata would burst into laughter, imagining the bewildered look on the warthog's face as it realized its mistake. But the funniest part of the story came when the warthog, in its haste to run out of the ambush site, ended up running head-on into the hunters, lifting one of them off the ground in the process.

Ade's laughter would echo through the trees as he recalled the chaotic scene that unfolded next. "Di warthog, e don forget di way back! E come dey rotate like Okro soup pot, and before we fit yarn Jack Robinson, e dey run straight back towards us!"

The image of the bewildered warthog careening back towards them, its eyes wide with panic, never failed to elicit raucous laughter from Aminata and the other listeners. "We dey look like akara wey fall for ground, everybody dey scatter!" Ade would exclaim, mimicking their frantic movements with exaggerated gestures.

"But di funniest part," Ade would continue, barely able to contain his amusement, "na when di warthog come lift Sule for ground like feather for breeze, and im skin cloth come unravel like yarn wey rat bite!"

The memory of poor Sule being lifted off the ground by the warthog's sheer momentum, his clothing unraveling in a comical fashion, was enough to send Aminata into fits of uncontrollable laughter. "Papa, you too much!" she would gasp between peals of laughter, tears streaming down her cheeks.

But the laughter didn't stop there. Ade would mimic the hunter's startled expression and the comical way he fell to the ground, his skin cloth unraveling and leaving him naked for all to see.

Abeni, who had heard the story countless times before, would join in the laughter, her eyes sparkling with amusement. "E be true, my dear. Sometimes, even the forest creatures fit teach us a lesson in humility."

And so, nestled beneath the shade of the baobab tree, Aminata and her family would revel in the absurdity of the forgetful warthog's misadventure, their laughter mingling with the rustle of the leaves and the gentle hum of the forest. It was moments like these that bound them together, weaving the fabric of their shared history and laughter into an unbreakable tapestry of love and joy.

• • • •

DESPITE THE CHALLENGES they faced, moments of love and togetherness were abundant in Aminata's family. They would gather around the fire in the evenings, sharing stories, jokes, and the simple joys of life. Abeni would often sing songs from their homeland, her voice carrying through the night like a gentle lullaby.

As they sat together, basking in the warmth of the fire and the love of family, Aminata felt a sense of peace and belonging wash over her. In those moments, she knew that no matter what the future held, she would always have the love and support of her family to guide her.

And so, under the vast canopy of stars and the watchful gaze of the moon, Aminata, Abeni, and Ade forged memories that would last a lifetime. Their bond was unbreakable, their love eternal, a beacon of hope and strength in a world filled with uncertainty.

The village itself was more than just a collection of huts and pathways; it was a living, breathing organism, pulsating with the rhythm of life. An extended family in its own right, the community was bound by a tapestry of tradition, mutual respect, and shared responsibilities. Here, in this tightly-knit enclave, every face was familiar, every voice a melody in the symphony of village life.

In the heart of the village, nestled beneath the protective canopy of ancient trees, the elders held court. Their wisdom, accumulated over decades of lived experience, was revered by all. Their weathered faces bore the traces of countless stories, each line etched with the weight of history. It was to them that the villagers turned for guidance and counsel, their words carrying the weight of authority and respect.

But the village was not just a sanctuary for the old; it was a cradle for the young, a place where children were cherished as the promise of tomorrow. They roamed the dusty pathways in packs, their laughter echoing through the air like the songs of birds. In their innocence lay the future of the community, a legacy waiting to be written in the annals of time.

Life in the village was punctuated by a calendar of festivals and ceremonies, each one a vibrant tapestry woven from the threads of culture and tradition. From the annual harvest festival to the rites of passage marking the transition from childhood to adulthood, these events served as anchors in the swirling currents of daily life.

During the harvest festival, the entire village would come together to give thanks to the gods for their bountiful blessings. Offerings of freshly harvested crops and livestock would be laid at the feet of the village shrine, accompanied by prayers and chants for a prosperous year ahead. As the sun dipped below the horizon, the villagers would gather around bonfires, their faces illuminated by the flickering flames, as they danced and sang late into the night.

Weddings were another highlight of village life, a joyous celebration of love and union. The air would be filled with the heady scent of perfumed oils and incense, as the bride and groom exchanged vows beneath a canopy of flowers and leaves. Festive feasts would be laid out, with tables groaning under the weight of sumptuous delicacies. And as the night wore on, the village would erupt in a cacophony of music and dance, as young and old alike joined hands in celebration.

But not all customs were cause for celebration; some were shrouded in superstition and fear. Among these was the practice of ostracizing individuals believed to be cursed or possessed by evil spirits. These unfortunate souls would be cast out from the village, forced to live on the fringes of society, their presence considered a harbinger of misfortune.

Despite the villagers' adherence to tradition, there were those who dared to challenge the status quo. They were the dissenting voices, the trailblazers who dared to question the wisdom of the elders. Their

actions often sparked heated debates and discord within the
community, as old beliefs clashed with new ideas.

Yet, amidst the tapestry of tradition and change, the village
remained a bastion of resilience and strength. Its people, bound
together by a common heritage and shared experiences, stood united in
the face of adversity, their spirits undaunted by the trials of life. And in
the heart of it all, Aminata found her place, a vibrant thread woven into
the rich fabric of village life.

8 Nature as a Teacher

• • • •

NATURE WAS NOT JUST a backdrop to Aminata's life; it was her classroom, her sanctuary, and her greatest teacher. From the lush forests to the winding rivers, from the soaring birds to the smallest insects, every aspect of the natural world held a lesson waiting to be learned.

For Aminata, the forest was a place of wonder and mystery, a realm where the ancient trees whispered secrets and the earth hummed with the rhythm of life. She would spend hours wandering through the dense undergrowth, her senses alert to every rustle and chirp. With each step, she learned to read the signs left by the creatures that called the forest home—the faint imprint of a hoof, the delicate tracery of a spider's web, and the scent of a predator lingering on the breeze.

Her father, Ade, was her guide in this verdant labyrinth, his knowledge of the forest as vast as the sky itself. He taught her to move with the stealth of a shadow, to listen to the heartbeat of the earth, and to respect the delicate balance of nature. Together, they would venture deep into the heart of the forest, their footsteps echoing in the dappled sunlight as they sought out the elusive treasures hidden within its depths.

The rivers that wound their way through the village were more than just sources of water; they were the lifeblood of the community, a constant presence in Aminata's daily life. She would spend hours playing in their cool, clear waters, diving beneath the surface to explore the hidden world below. The river was her playground, her refuge, and her greatest teacher.

From the river, Aminata learned the importance of adaptability and resilience. She watched as the water flowed inexorably downstream, bending and twisting around obstacles in its path. She saw how even the mightiest boulders were worn away by the relentless force of the current, their rough edges smoothed into submission. And she understood that, like the river, she too must learn to navigate the twists and turns of life with grace and determination.

But perhaps the greatest lessons came from the creatures that shared her world—the animals that roamed the forest, the birds that soared through the sky, and the insects that buzzed among the flowers. Each creature had its own story to tell, its own unique perspective on life and survival.

Aminata marveled at the grace and agility of the antelope as it bounded through the underbrush, its slender legs carrying it effortlessly over fallen logs and tangled roots. She watched in awe as the birds of prey soared high above the canopy, their keen eyes scanning the forest floor for signs of movement. And she laughed with delight at the antics of the mischievous monkeys, their playful chatter echoing through the trees.

For Aminata, her connection to nature was more than just practical; it was deeply spiritual. She felt a sense of kinship with the earth, a recognition of her place in the intricate web of life. She saw herself not as separate from nature, but as an integral part of it—a leaf on the same branch, a drop in the same river.

In the quiet moments spent beneath the canopy of trees, Aminata would commune with the spirits of the forest, feeling their presence in the rustle of leaves and the gentle sigh of the wind. She would offer prayers of gratitude to the earth, thanking it for its bounty and its beauty. And she would listen, with an open heart and a humble spirit, to the wisdom whispered on the breeze.

In nature, Aminata found not just knowledge, but wisdom. She learned to see the world through eyes unclouded by ego or ambition, to appreciate the beauty and complexity of life in all its forms. And she understood, perhaps more deeply than most, that she was but a small part of a vast and wondrous universe—a universe that held secrets beyond imagining, and lessons beyond measure.

. . . .

FROM A YOUNG AGE, AMINATA had a spirit of adventure. She was always eager to explore, to see what lay beyond the next hill or across the river. Her curiosity knew no bounds, and her parents encouraged this trait, recognizing it as a sign of her intelligence and vitality.

Aminata's adventures often led her to new discoveries. She would find hidden streams, secret groves, and places where the forest seemed to hold its breath, as if waiting for her to uncover its secrets. She collected stones, feathers, and other treasures, each one a reminder of her journeys and the wonders she had encountered.

Her spirit of adventure was not just about physical exploration but about learning and growth. She was always asking questions, eager to understand

Her spirit of adventure was not just about physical exploration but about learning and growth. She was always asking questions, eager to understand the why and how of everything she encountered. Her inquisitiveness was both endearing and exhausting to her parents, who found themselves constantly explaining the mysteries of the world to their bright-eyed daughter.

Aminata's adventures often brought her into contact with the village's wise elders. These were men and women who had lived long, full lives and were repositories of knowledge and tradition. They welcomed her curiosity and took pleasure in sharing their wisdom with her. Aminata learned about the medicinal properties of plants, the significance of the stars in the night sky, and the ancient stories that shaped their culture.

One elder in particular, Baba, took a special interest in Aminata. Baba was a man of great age and dignity, his face lined with the marks of time and experience. His eyes, though dim with age, sparkled with intelligence and humor. He was known for his vast knowledge of the natural world and his deep understanding of the spiritual realm.

Baba would often take Aminata on walks through the forest, pointing out plants and animals and explaining their significance. He taught her how to listen to the whispers of the wind, the songs of the birds, and the rustling of the leaves. He showed her how to feel the pulse of the earth beneath her feet and to sense the presence of unseen spirits.

"Aminata," he would say, his voice a gentle rumble, "the world is full of magic and mystery. Never lose your sense of wonder. Always be open to learning, and you will find that the world has much to teach you."

Aminata treasured these moments with Baba. His teachings resonated deeply with her, fueling her curiosity and deepening her connection to the natural world. She felt a profound sense of gratitude for his guidance and wisdom, knowing that he was helping to shape her into a person of depth and understanding.

Life in the village followed the rhythms of nature, the changing seasons dictating the pace of daily activities. There was a time for planting and a time for harvesting, a time for celebration and a time for rest. The villagers moved in harmony with these rhythms, their lives intertwined with the cycles of the earth.

Aminata loved the changing seasons, each one bringing its own unique beauty and challenges. The rainy season transformed the landscape into a lush, green paradise, the rivers swelling with life-giving water. The dry season brought a different kind of beauty, the golden grasses waving in the breeze, the sky a brilliant, cloudless blue.

Each season had its own rituals and traditions. During the planting season, the villagers would hold ceremonies to honor the earth and ask for bountiful crops. The harvest season was a time of great celebration, with feasts, dances, and songs of gratitude. Aminata participated in these rituals with enthusiasm, her heart swelling with pride and joy to be part of such a rich and vibrant culture.

Aminata's place in the community was secure, her presence bringing joy and hope to those around her. She was loved and cherished by all, her bright spirit and infectious laughter a source of happiness. She was known for her kindness and generosity, always willing to help others and share what she had.

The community's embrace was a source of strength and comfort for Aminata. She knew that she was never alone, that there were always people around her who cared for her and would support her. This sense of belonging gave her the confidence to explore, to learn, and to grow, secure in the knowledge that she was part of a larger whole.

• • • •

LIFE IN THE VILLAGE, though filled with moments of joy and wonder, was not immune to the trials and tribulations that plagued humanity. Adversity, like a relentless shadow, lurked at the edges of their existence, waiting to pounce at the slightest hint of weakness. And so, despite the idyllic nature of her early years, Aminata soon learned that hardship was an unavoidable companion on the journey of life.

The first signs of adversity often manifested in the form of nature's wrath. Droughts, like merciless predators, stalked the land, sucking the very life from the soil and leaving behind a barren wasteland. The villagers, whose lives were intricately woven with the rhythms of the earth, felt the sting of each parched blade of grass and withered leaf.

During one particularly harsh drought, the village teetered on the brink of extinction, its people wilting like flowers denied the nourishment of rain. The crops withered in the fields, their shriveled husks a bitter reminder of the fragility of life. Water became a precious commodity, more valuable than gold, and every drop was hoarded like a precious jewel.

But nature's fury was not the only foe the village faced. Diseases, like silent assassins, crept through their midst, claiming victims with merciless efficiency. Fever, cough, and delirium spread like wildfire, leaving a trail of death and despair in their wake. The villagers, whose knowledge of medicine was limited to the healing properties of herbs and potions, watched helplessly as their loved ones succumbed to the ravages of sickness.

One particularly virulent disease, known locally as *Dume* "the silent killer," struck fear into the hearts of the villagers. Its victims would waste away before their very eyes, their bodies consumed by an unseen enemy. Mothers wept for their children, husbands for their wives, as the village descended into a state of mourning and despair.

Yet, even in the darkest of times, humor found a way to weave its thread through the tapestry of despair. There was the story of old Kofi, a cantankerous elder whose appetite rivaled that of a hungry lion. When food became scarce during the height of the drought, Kofi's belly rumbled like distant thunder, his hunger gnawing at him like a ravenous beast.

In a moment of desperation, Kofi, driven to the brink of madness by hunger, decided to take matters into his own hands. With a grim determination, he reached for his treasured cloak, a prized possession fashioned from the hide of a sacred cow. But instead of wrapping himself in its warm embrace, he tore off a strip and, with a resigned sigh, began to chew on it like a piece of tough meat.

The sight of the venerable elder gnawing on his own garment like a starving goat sent ripples of laughter through the village, a welcome respite from the grim reality of their plight. And though Kofi's actions may have been born out of desperation, they served as a reminder that even in the face of adversity, there was still room for laughter and camaraderie.

In the crucible of adversity, the villagers of Aminata's community forged bonds of resilience and unity that were stronger than steel. They faced nature's wrath and the scourge of disease with courage and determination, refusing to be cowed by the specter of despair. And though the road ahead was fraught with uncertainty, they marched forward with heads held high, their spirits unbroken and their resolve unshaken. For in the end, it was not the challenges they faced that defined them, but their unwavering determination to overcome them, come what may.

One of the most difficult trials to befall Aminata's family and the village was the sudden illness that befell her mother, Abeni. Abeni, a pillar of strength and vitality in the community, was suddenly stricken by a mysterious ailment that left her weak and bedridden. The news sent shockwaves through the village, as whispers of concern and fear rippled through the tightly-knit community.

Aminata, who had always looked up to her mother as a source of wisdom and guidance, was devastated by the news. She watched helplessly as Abeni, who had always been the picture of health, grew weaker with each passing day. Yet despite her fear and uncertainty, Aminata remained steadfast by her mother's side, offering whatever comfort and support she could.

In a desperate bid to find a cure for Abeni's illness, the village elders summoned the healer, a wise and revered figure whose knowledge of herbs and potions was legendary. The healer arrived amidst a flurry of whispered prayers and hopeful expectations, his weathered face set in a mask of solemn determination.

Aminata watched as the healer examined her mother, his hands moving with practiced precision as he felt for signs of illness. He muttered incantations under his breath, his words a whispered plea to the spirits of the earth for guidance and insight. And then, with a solemn nod, he set to work, mixing together a potent concoction of herbs and roots, his wrinkled hands moving with the grace of a dancer.

For Aminata, the days blurred together in a haze of fear and uncertainty. She spent every waking moment by her mother's side, her heart heavy with worry. She held Abeni's hand, whispered words of comfort, and tended to her every need with a devotion that bordered on obsession.

As the healer's remedies began to take effect, Aminata watched with bated breath as her mother's strength slowly returned. It was a gradual process, marked by small victories and setbacks, but with each passing day, Abeni grew stronger, her spirit unbroken by the trials she had endured.

But while Aminata remained steadfast in her devotion to her mother, her father, Ade, struggled to come to terms with the gravity of the situation. Ade, who had always been the rock of the family, found himself adrift in a sea of fear and uncertainty. He watched helplessly as the woman he loved with all his heart lay bedridden before him, her once vibrant spirit dimmed by the shadow of illness.

For Ade, Abeni's illness was a test of faith and endurance. He spent sleepless nights by her side, his heart heavy with worry and despair. He prayed to the gods for her recovery, offering sacrifices of fruit and grain in the hopes of appeasing their wrath. And when his prayers were answered, and Abeni's strength began to return, he wept tears of relief and gratitude, his faith in the power of love and perseverance renewed.

But even as Abeni's health improved, whispers of suspicion and superstition lingered in the air. Rumors spread like wildfire through the village, fueled by fear and uncertainty. Some whispered of a witch, a dark and malevolent presence lurking in the shadows, her eyes burning with an otherworldly fire. It was believed that she had brought misfortune upon the village.

This witch, so the rumors went, lived in a secluded hut on the outskirts of the village, her presence a source of dread and unease. Children whispered tales of her strange appearance and eerie demeanor, their imaginations running wild with fear. And though no one dared to venture too close to her dwelling, the mere mention of her name was enough to send shivers down their spines.

Abeni's illness was a stark reminder of the fragility of life and the power of love and resilience to overcome even the greatest of challenges. It tested the bonds of family and community, pushing them to the brink of despair and then pulling them back with the promise of hope and renewal. And though the shadow of illness may have darkened their doorstep, it was ultimately the light of love and unity that shone through, illuminating their path forward with the promise of a brighter tomorrow.

••••

ADE, MEANWHILE, CONTINUED to be a pillar of strength for Aminata. Despite the worries and challenges they faced, he remained a steadfast source of support and guidance. He continued to teach Aminata the skills and knowledge she would need to navigate the world, instilling in her a deep sense of confidence and self-reliance.

One of the most important lessons Ade imparted to Aminata was the value of wisdom and discernment. He taught her to think critically, to question and analyze, and to seek out the truth. He encouraged her to be curious and open-minded, to always be willing to learn and grow.

"Aminata," he would say, "knowledge is the greatest treasure you can possess. It will guide you, protect you, and help you make wise decisions. Never stop seeking it."

Ade's teachings left a lasting impression on Aminata. She grew up with a thirst for knowledge and a deep respect for wisdom. She understood that learning was a lifelong journey, one that would continue to enrich and shape her life.

12 New Life Beginnings

• • • •

AS AMINATA GREW, SO did her responsibilities. She took on more tasks around the home and the village, helping to tend the garden, fetch water, and care for the younger children. She embraced these responsibilities with enthusiasm, seeing them as opportunities to learn and contribute to her community.

Her parents continued to be her primary teachers, but she also learned from the other villagers. The women taught her how to weave baskets, prepare traditional dishes, and perform the rituals and ceremonies that were so integral to their culture. The men showed her how to build and repair structures, hunt and fish, and protect their village.

Aminata's days were full and rewarding. She thrived on the sense of purpose and accomplishment that came from her work. She took pride in her skills and knowledge, and she was eager to continue learning and growing.

As Aminata approached adolescence, she began to notice changes within herself. She was growing taller and stronger, her body beginning to take on the curves and contours of womanhood. She felt a new awareness of herself and the world around her, a heightened sensitivity to the beauty and complexity of life.

These changes brought with them new challenges and opportunities. Aminata found herself grappling with questions about her identity, her place in the world, and her future. She sought guidance from her parents and the elders, who reassured her that these feelings were a natural part of growing up.

Abeni, in particular, was a source of comfort and wisdom during this time. She shared her own experiences of growing up, helping Aminata to navigate the confusing and often overwhelming emotions of adolescence. She taught her daughter about the cycles of life, the ebb and flow of change, and the importance of staying true to oneself.

As Aminata stood on the threshold of adolescence, she felt a sense of excitement and anticipation for the future. She knew that there would be challenges and hardships, but she also knew that she was well-prepared to face them. She had the love and support of her family, the wisdom of her elders, and the strength and resilience she had inherited from her ancestors.

. . . .

THE VILLAGE CONTINUED to thrive, its rhythms and cycles a constant source of stability and continuity. Aminata took comfort in the knowledge that she was part of a long and proud lineage, a community that valued tradition, wisdom, and love.

Aminata's early years had laid a strong foundation for her future. She had learned to cherish the beauty and mystery of the natural world, to respect the wisdom of her elders, and to value the importance of family and community. She had faced challenges with courage and resilience, growing stronger and wiser with each experience.

As she looked to the future, Aminata felt a sense of hope and determination. She knew that her journey was just beginning, that there were many more adventures and lessons ahead. She was ready to embrace the challenges and opportunities that lay before her, guided by the values and teachings of her parents and the community she loved.

Aminata's story was one of resilience, love, and hope. It was a story of a young girl growing up under the protective canopy of the baobab tree, nurtured by the wisdom and strength of her parents and the embrace of her community. Yet, like all stories, it was one that would soon face new and unforeseen challenges.

13 Departure

· · · ·

THE DAY DAWNED LIKE any other in the village, with the sun casting its golden rays across the landscape and the birds singing their morning songs. But as Aminata watched her father, Ade, prepare to depart for his hunt, a sense of unease settled in the pit of her stomach like a stone.

Ade, the village's best hunter and a man of great wisdom, moved with his usual grace and confidence. Yet, as he shouldered his bow and quiver, Aminata couldn't shake the feeling that something was amiss. She noticed the way the leaves rustled in the wind, whispering secrets that she couldn't decipher, and the way the birds flew in erratic patterns, as if trying to warn of impending danger.

Abeni, too, felt a strange emptiness gnawing at her heart as she watched her husband depart. It was a feeling she couldn't shake, a sense of foreboding that lingered like a shadow at the edge of her vision. But she pushed the thought away, chiding herself for succumbing to superstition.

As Ade and his fellow hunters ventured deeper into the forest, strange signs began to manifest themselves, like omens of impending doom. A black crow perched ominously on a branch, its piercing gaze following their every move. A sudden gust of wind sent leaves swirling in a chaotic dance, as if the forest itself was writhing in anticipation.

But Ade paid no heed to these signs, his mind focused on the task at hand. He moved with the confidence of a man who had spent his life in harmony with the wild, his senses attuned to the rhythms of the forest. Yet, even he couldn't shake the feeling of unease that settled like a heavy shroud over the landscape.

· · · ·

IT WAS MIDDAY WHEN tragedy struck, shattering the tranquility of the forest like a thunderclap. Ade, in pursuit of a wild boar, found himself face to face with the creature, its tusks gleaming in the dappled sunlight. In the blink of an eye, the situation escalated into a deadly confrontation, as man and beast clashed in a desperate struggle for survival.

Despite Ade's skill and bravery, the boar proved to be a formidable adversary. With a swift and unexpected charge, it gored him with its razor-sharp tusks, leaving him gravely injured and incapacitated. The hunters, stunned by the sudden turn of events, rushed to Ade's aid, but it was already too late.

As Ade lay bleeding on the forest floor, his companions realized the extent of his injuries. With heavy hearts, they made the agonizing decision to abandon the hunt and carry their fallen comrade back to the village. The journey seemed interminable, each step a painful reminder of the loss that awaited them.

• • • •

BACK IN THE VILLAGE, Abeni waited with bated breath for her husband's return, her heart filled with a sense of dread she couldn't explain. When the hunters finally emerged from the forest, carrying Ade's lifeless body on a makeshift stretcher, her worst fears were realized in an instant.

The news of Ade's death spread like wildfire through the village, casting a pall of sorrow over the community. But for Abeni, the pain of loss cut deeper than any blade. She clung to her daughter, Aminata, seeking solace in the warmth of their embrace, but the void left by Ade's absence seemed insurmountable.

• • • •

AMINATA WAS DEVASTATED by her father's death. Ade had been her hero, her teacher, and her protector. His absence left a void in her heart that seemed impossible to fill. She cried for days, her young heart breaking with the weight of her grief.

Abeni, though equally heartbroken, remained a pillar of strength for her daughter. She comforted Aminata, holding her close and whispering words of solace. She told stories of Ade, reminding Aminata of his bravery, wisdom, and love. These stories, once a source of joy, now became a means of healing, helping Aminata to remember her father not with sorrow, but with gratitude for the time they had shared.

The village rallied around Abeni and Aminata, offering support and comfort. In the ceremony conducted to honor Ade's spirit and ensure his peaceful journey to the afterlife, the village elders led solemn rituals steeped in tradition and reverence. They gathered around Ade's body, adorned with sacred herbs and symbols of his prowess as a hunter, and offered prayers to the spirits of the earth and sky.

The healer, wielding his knowledge of herbs and incantations, performed rituals to purify Ade's spirit and guide him safely to the realm of the ancestors. Offerings of food, drink, and precious items were laid at his feet, symbols of respect and tribute to his life and legacy.

As the sun dipped below the horizon and the stars twinkled overhead, the villagers joined together in song and dance, their voices rising in a haunting melody that echoed through the night. It was a time of mourning and remembrance, but also of celebration, as they honored Ade's memory and celebrated his journey to the afterlife.

Throughout the ceremony, Abeni and Aminata stood at the forefront, their grief mingling with gratitude for the love and support of their community. Together, they bore witness to the final farewell to a beloved husband, father, and friend, their hearts heavy with sorrow but filled with the hope of reunion in the spirit world.

The death of Ade, the village's best hunter and beloved patriarch, marked the end of an era for Aminata and her family. It was a loss that reverberated through the community, leaving behind a void that could never be filled. And though the pain of his passing would linger like

a scar on their hearts, they would carry on, drawing strength from the
memories of a man whose spirit would live on in the hearts of all who
knew and loved him.

As the months passed and Aminata and her mother, Abeni, began to heal from the loss of Ade, their lives slowly regained a semblance of normalcy. However, beneath the surface of this fragile peace, a new and more insidious threat was beginning to take shape. Ade's brother, Kofi, who had always been a distant and somewhat sinister figure, started appearing more frequently around their home.

Kofi had always been a man of dubious morals and intentions. His presence was often accompanied by an unsettling air that made people uneasy. His dark eyes, which now seemed to linger too long on Aminata, began to betray a hidden, dangerous intent. His behavior shifted subtly at first, small gestures and comments that seemed harmless but left Aminata feeling uncomfortable and unsafe.

One afternoon, as Aminata was helping her mother with the chores, Kofi arrived unexpectedly. His entrance was abrupt, almost forceful, and the atmosphere in the hut grew tense. Aminata noticed the way his eyes roved around, finally settling on her with an intensity that made her skin crawl.

"Kofi, what you dey do here?" Abeni asked, her voice a mix of surprise and suspicion.

"I just come see how una dey," Kofi replied, his tone overly casual. "Since Ade no dey again, I wan help una small."

Abeni forced a smile and nodded, though Aminata could see the wariness in her eyes. She couldn't shake off the feeling that Kofi's intentions were far from altruistic.

As the weeks went by, Kofi's visits became more frequent. He often found excuses to be alone with Aminata, his presence becoming increasingly invasive.

• • • •

ONE EVENING, WHEN ABENI had gone to gather herbs in the forest, Kofi seized the opportunity to act on his dark desires.

Aminata was in the kitchen, preparing the evening meal, when Kofi walked in. His steps were slow, deliberate, and she felt a shiver run down her spine. He stood in the doorway, blocking her only exit.

"Ah, Aminata," he began, his voice low and unsettling. "You don grow into fine woman. Your papa no go ever forgive me if I no take care of you well."

Aminata forced a polite smile, hoping to diffuse the situation. "Thank you, Uncle. I dey okay. Mama dey take care of me well well."

Kofi moved closer, his eyes narrowing. "You need more than just your mama, Aminata. You need a man to protect you."

Aminata's heart raced as she backed away, but Kofi continued to advance, his intentions becoming clearer with each step. "Uncle, I fit manage. Abeg, make you leave me."

He ignored her plea, his hand reaching out to touch her arm. Aminata recoiled, her fear turning into a surge of adrenaline. "Stop am!" she shouted, her voice trembling.

Kofi's face twisted into a sinister grin. "You no fit tell me wetin to do," he said, his grip tightening. "You be woman now. Time don reach to know the ways of a man."

Panic surged through Aminata as she struggled to free herself. "Mama! Mama!" she screamed, knowing her mother was too far to hear her cries.

Desperation fueled her strength. She twisted and turned, finally breaking free from Kofi's grasp. She dashed towards the corner of the kitchen where a small knife lay on the table. She grabbed it, her hands shaking, and turned to face him, brandishing the blade with as much courage as she could muster.

Kofi laughed, a dark, humorless sound that sent chills down her spine. "You think say you fit use that for me?" he taunted, stepping forward.

Aminata's grip tightened on the knife. "If you no comot now, I go use am," she threatened, her voice steadier than she felt.

For a moment, Kofi hesitated, his eyes flickering with uncertainty. But his desire overcame his caution, and he lunged at her. In a flash of instinct, Aminata thrust the knife forward, striking him in the groin.

Kofi let out a howl of pain, doubling over and clutching at his wound. Aminata didn't wait to see the extent of the damage. She darted past him and fled from the hut, her heart pounding in her chest.

• • • •

SHE RAN THROUGH THE village, tears streaming down her face, until she found herself at the edge of the forest. Her legs finally gave way, and she collapsed, sobbing uncontrollably.

Minutes later, Abeni stumbled upon her there. Having heard about the commotion from the neighbors, she had rushed out to find her. She dropped to her knees beside her daughter, gathering her into her arms. "Aminata, wetin happen? Wetin Kofi do?"

Between sobs, Aminata recounted the horrifying events. Abeni's face hardened with a mix of fury and fear as she listened. "That man no go ever touch you again," she vowed, her voice shaking with anger. "We go find way to protect ourselves."

The following days were filled with tension and unease. Kofi had disappeared from the village, nursing his injury and plotting his next move. The villagers whispered about the incident, their suspicion and fear growing.

Abeni knew they had to act quickly. She gathered the women of the village, explaining what had happened and seeking their support. "We no fit let this man terrorize us," she declared. "We must stand together."

The women, outraged and determined, agreed to help. They kept a close watch on their homes and families, ready to defend themselves if necessary. The village healer was also brought into the fold, providing protective charms and herbs to ward off any further attacks.

• • • •

ONE EVENING, AS THE sun set and the village gathered around the communal fire, Abeni addressed the elders. "Kofi don show say he be danger to this community. We must banish am before he cause more harm."

The elders, though initially reluctant, were swayed by the collective voice of the women and the undeniable evidence of Kofi's actions. It was decided that Kofi would be confronted and given the choice to leave the village peacefully or face the consequences of his actions.

Kofi, cornered and with no allies left, chose to leave. His departure was met with a mixture of relief and lingering fear, but the village knew they had done the right thing. They had protected their own and upheld their values of safety and respect.

In the aftermath, Aminata and Abeni began to rebuild their lives. The trauma of the attack lingered, but they drew strength from each other and their community. Abeni continued to teach Aminata the ways of their ancestors, instilling in her the resilience and courage that had seen them through the darkest times.

Aminata learned that strength wasn't just about physical power but also about the support of those around her. She understood that her community, despite its flaws, was a source of immense strength and protection. And she vowed never to let fear control her life again.

• • • •

AS THE VILLAGE SETTLED back into its rhythm, Aminata found solace in the routines that had once brought her joy. She returned to the forest, her sanctuary, and the place where she felt most connected to her father's spirit. She continued to learn and grow, her experiences shaping her into a young woman of remarkable resilience and wisdom.

Through it all, the bond between Aminata and her mother grew stronger. They had faced unimaginable challenges and had come out the other side, scarred but unbroken. Together, they honored the memory of Ade, their protector and guide, and looked to the future with hope and determination.

And so, life in the village continued, a mixture of joy and sorrow, of resilience and unity. Aminata carried the lessons of her childhood with her, ready to face whatever challenges lay ahead, knowing she had the strength of her family and community behind her.

15 The Return of a Dark Past

AS TIME WENT ON, AMINATA and Abeni began to find a semblance of peace in their lives. The departure of Kofi had lifted a heavy shadow from their home, and the village once again felt like a safe place. Aminata continued her education in the ways of her ancestors, drawing strength from the natural world and the community around her. She and her mother had grown even closer, their bond fortified by the trials they had endured together.

However, the peace they enjoyed was fragile. Unbeknownst to them, Kofi's departure marked the beginning of a new chapter of darkness that would eventually circle back to them.

Kofi's departure from the village was far from smooth. With a wound that had only partially healed and no place to call home, he found survival a daily struggle. He roamed from village to village, but word of his misdeeds had traveled ahead of him. Communities turned him away, unwilling to harbor someone with such a tainted reputation.

Hungry and desperate, Kofi eventually stumbled upon a group of men gathered around a campfire deep in the forest. They were a rough-looking bunch, their faces hardened by a life of crime and violence. These men were slave hunters and bandits, known for terrorizing villages and capturing people to sell into slavery.

With nowhere else to turn, Kofi joined their ranks. His moral descent was swift and brutal. He quickly proved himself to be ruthless, his bitterness and anger fueling his actions. He took part in raiding villages, rounding up men, women, and children to be sold as slaves, and looting whatever they could carry. Kofi's brutality became notorious, and stories of his atrocities spread far and wide.

• • • •

THE TALES OF KOFI'S new life eventually reached Aminata's village. Whispers and rumors swirled among the villagers, each story more horrifying than the last. At first, Aminata and Abeni refused to believe that Kofi, their own flesh and blood, could have sunk to such depths of depravity. But the stories were consistent, and the details too specific to dismiss.

One evening, as Aminata and Abeni sat by the fire, a group of elders approached their home. Their faces were grave, and Aminata felt a knot of dread form in her stomach. She knew they brought news, and she feared what it might be.

"Abeni, Aminata," one of the elders began, his voice heavy with sorrow, "we have heard terrible news about Kofi."

• • • •

ABENI'S FACE PALED, but she remained silent, waiting for the elder to continue.

"He has become a slave hunter," the elder said. "He and his group have been raiding villages, capturing our people and selling them into slavery."

Abeni's eyes filled with tears, but she held her head high. "This man is no longer part of our family," she said firmly. "We disowned him when he brought shame upon us."

Aminata felt a mix of emotions—anger, sorrow, and a deep sense of betrayal. She could not understand how someone from their family could commit such heinous acts. The elders left, leaving Aminata and Abeni to grapple with the horrifying news.

• • • •

AS THE DAYS PASSED, more stories of Kofi's atrocities reached the village. The elders convened a council to discuss the growing threat. They feared that Kofi's band might eventually target their village, seeking revenge for his banishment.

"We must prepare," one of the elders said. "We need to fortify our defenses and protect our people."

The villagers rallied together, strengthening their homes and preparing for the worst. They set up watchtowers and organized patrols to keep an eye out for any signs of Kofi's band. The sense of community that had always been their strength now became their shield against the looming threat.

• • • •

ABENI WAS DEEPLY TROUBLED by the news of her brother-in-law's actions. She felt a heavy burden of guilt and responsibility, though she knew there was nothing she could have done to prevent Kofi's descent into darkness. She focused on protecting her daughter and her village, determined to stand strong against any threat.

One night, as Aminata and Abeni sat together in their home, Abeni spoke of her feelings. "Aminata, my child, I am deeply saddened by what Kofi has become. But we must not let his actions define us. We must stay strong and protect our village."

Aminata nodded, her resolve matching her mother's. "We will, Mama. We will stand together and face whatever comes our way."

. . . .

THE DREADED DAY FINALLY arrived. One early morning, a scout rushed into the village, breathless and panicked. "They are coming!" he shouted. "Kofi's band is approaching!"

The village erupted into action. Men and women armed themselves with whatever they could find—bows, spears, and makeshift weapons. The children were hurriedly taken to a hidden area, away from the impending danger.

Aminata and Abeni prepared themselves as well. Abeni took a deep breath and looked at her daughter. "Remember what I have taught you, Aminata. Be brave and stay strong."

Aminata nodded, gripping her spear tightly. The sounds of approaching footsteps and voices grew louder. The tension in the air was palpable.

Kofi and his men entered the village, their eyes gleaming with malice. He headed straight to Ade's homestead. Kofi's face was a twisted mask of anger and resentment. "So, this is how you welcome your family," he sneered, looking directly at Abeni.

"You are no family of ours," Abeni retorted, her voice steady. "You lost that right the day you betrayed us."

Kofi laughed, a cold, mirthless sound. "You think you can stand against me? Against us?"

Abeni stood her ground. "We will defend our village. We will not let you take our people."

· · · ·

THE CONFRONTATION QUICKLY escalated into a violent clash. The villagers fought bravely, their determination fueled by the need to protect their homes and loved ones. Aminata found herself face-to-face with Kofi, her heart pounding in her chest.

"You think you can defeat me, little girl?" Kofi taunted, his eyes filled with hatred.

Aminata's grip on her spear tightened. "I will protect my family and my village," she replied, her voice unwavering.

A fierce struggle ensued. Kofi, using his strength, tried to overpower Aminata. She fought back with all her might, but Kofi's experience and brute force began to take a toll. In the midst of their struggle, one of the bandits was speared by a villager and fell right outside their door.

Aminata's mother, Abeni, saw the struggle and without hesitation, she jumped in to save her daughter. The sight of her mother gave Aminata a surge of hope and strength. Abeni grabbed a piece of wood and swung it at Kofi. It got him squarely on the head momentarily staggering him.

"Leave her alone, Kofi!" Abeni screamed, her voice filled with both anger and desperation.

Kofi, enraged by the interference and pain, pushed Abeni away forcefully. In the chaos, Kofi's spear, which had been swinging wildly, found Abeni's side. The moment seemed to stretch out, time slowing as the horror of the scene unfolded. Kofi's face contorted with shock and horror as he realized what he had done.

"No!" Kofi shouted, his voice breaking. He had never intended to harm his Abeni.

Abeni staggered, her hands clutching the wound. She looked at Kofi with a mixture of pain and sadness before collapsing to the ground.

"Mama!" Aminata screamed, rushing to her mother's side.

Abeni's breathing was shallow, and her eyes were filled with tears. "Aminata... be strong... I love you..." she whispered, her voice barely audible.

Aminata sobbed, holding her mother's hand as life slipped away from Abeni's body. The village was in turmoil, the sounds of battle fading into the background as Aminata's world fell apart.

· · · ·

IN THE CHAOS AND HEARTBREAK, the bandits took advantage of the situation. Aminata, weakened by grief and shock, was captured. They tied her up, her struggles feeble against their strength.

Kofi stood there, paralyzed by what he had done. Abeni, the one person who had still held a place in his heart despite everything, lay dead because of him. The bandits, seeing his hesitation, dragged Aminata away.

"Kofi, we need to go!" one of the bandits shouted, pulling him from his stupor.

As they retreated, Kofi looked back at the village. The place that had once been his home was now a scene of devastation. The faces of the villagers, filled with anger and sorrow, burned into his memory.

Aminata, bound and gagged, was thrown over a horse. She looked back at her mother's lifeless body, tears streaming down her face. The pain in her heart was unbearable, the loss of her mother an unimaginable void.

The bandits rode away, leaving behind a village in mourning. Aminata's cries of sorrow were muffled by the gag, her body trembling with grief and fear. Kofi rode in silence, his mind a whirlwind of guilt and despair. He had become the monster he once feared, and now there was no turning back. The other slaves were bundled into a makeshift prison-carriage pulled by horses.

17 Shock & Aftermath

• • • •

AS THE DUST SETTLED and the bandits disappeared into the distance, a heart-wrenching silence fell over the village. The once lively and vibrant community was now a scene of utter devastation. Many villagers lay lifeless, their bodies scattered among the ruins of their homes. Those who had survived the initial attack walked among the fallen, their faces etched with shock and disbelief.

The elders, their hearts heavy with sorrow, took charge of the grim task of gathering the dead. There were too many to bury individually, so they dug mass graves, placing the bodies side by side. The air was thick with the scent of earth and death, and the mournful wails of the villagers filled the sky. Gloom and despair hung over the village like a dark cloud, suffocating the spirit of hope that once thrived there.

Aminata's friends and neighbors wept openly, their cries a chorus of grief. The loss of so many loved ones was an unbearable weight, and the reality of their absence sank in like a cold blade. Parents mourned their children, siblings clung to each other in shared sorrow, and the village felt an indescribable emptiness. The horrors of the raid had left an indelible mark on their hearts, and the pain of loss was a constant, throbbing presence.

• • • •

MEANWHILE, THOSE WHO had been captured were herded together like animals. They were tied up with coarse ropes, their wrists bound so tightly that the skin was raw and bleeding. Fear and uncertainty were etched into their faces as they were forced into a makeshift prison carriage—an iron cage mounted on a wooden cart, pulled by horses. The captives huddled together, seeking comfort in the closeness of others, but their eyes were wide with terror.

Aminata, among the captured, felt numbness settle over her. The image of her mother's lifeless body haunted her thoughts, and the weight of her loss was almost too much to bear. Her wrists ached from the tight bindings, and every jolt of the carriage sent a fresh wave of pain through her body. The sound of the horses' hooves clattering against the ground was a constant reminder of their captivity and their unknown fate.

* * * *

BACK IN THE VILLAGE, the aftermath of the raid was a sight of utter devastation. The elders did their best to comfort the survivors, but their own hearts were heavy with grief. They organized the burials, placing flowers and tokens of remembrance on the mass graves. The rituals, usually a source of solace and closure, felt hollow in the face of such overwhelming loss.

Abeni's death was particularly hard for the villagers to bear. She had been a pillar of strength, a source of wisdom and kindness. Her passing left a void that could never be filled. The village women wept as they washed her body, preparing it for burial with the utmost care and respect. They adorned her with her favorite beads and wrapped her in a shroud, whispering prayers for her peaceful journey to the afterlife.

The survivors gathered around the graves, their tears mingling with the freshly turned earth. They sang mournful songs, their voices quivering with emotion. The air was thick with the scent of incense and the sound of wailing, a testament to the depth of their sorrow. The village had been through dark times before, but this was unlike anything they had ever experienced. The sheer scale of the loss was overwhelming, and the path to healing seemed impossibly long.

Among the mourners were children who had lost parents, parents who had lost children, and friends who had lost each other. The weight of their despair was palpable, and the future seemed bleak. They held each other close, seeking comfort in shared grief, but the pain of loss was a constant companion. The once tight-knit community was now a shadow of its former self, struggling to find a way forward in the wake of such tragedy.

· · · ·

THE CAPTIVES, INCLUDING Aminata, were transported through dense forests and across barren landscapes. The journey was grueling, and the constant fear of what lay ahead gnawed at their hearts. They were given little food and water, their basic needs barely met. The bandits showed no mercy, treating them with contempt and cruelty.

Aminata's mind was a whirlwind of emotions. She thought of her mother, of her village, and of the life she had known. The uncertainty of her future was terrifying. She could not fathom what awaited them at the end of this journey, and the fear of the unknown was a constant, gnawing presence.

In the carriage, the captives whispered to each other, trying to make sense of their situation. "Where do you think they are taking us?" one of the older men asked, his voice trembling with fear.

"I don't know," another replied, "but it can't be anywhere good. We must stay strong, for each other."

Aminata listened to their words, drawing a small measure of comfort from their solidarity. She knew that whatever lay ahead, they would face it together. The bond of shared suffering was a fragile thread of hope in the darkness of their captivity.

. . . .

KOFI RODE IN SILENCE, his mind a storm of conflicting emotions. The realization of what he had done weighed heavily on him. The image of Abeni's lifeless body haunted his thoughts, a constant reminder of his actions. He had never intended to harm her, but in his rage and desperation, he had become the monster he once feared.

The bandits, seeing his hesitation, urged him to keep moving. They had no time for remorse or second thoughts. They were focused on their mission, their minds set on the profit they would make from selling the captives. Kofi, torn between his guilt and his fear, followed them, his heart heavy with the burden of his sins.

. . . .

AS THE DAYS PASSED, the captives grew weaker, their spirits battered by the harsh conditions and the constant fear. Aminata clung to the memories of her mother and her village, drawing strength from the love and warmth they had shared. She vowed to stay strong, to survive whatever lay ahead, and to honor her mother's memory by never giving up.

The bandits, focused on their mission, pushed forward relentlessly. The journey was grueling, the nights cold and the days scorching. The captives huddled together for warmth, sharing what little food and water they were given. Their bonds grew stronger with each passing day, their shared suffering a source of solidarity and strength.

One night, as the captives lay huddled together, Aminata found herself next to an elderly woman. The woman's face was lined with age and hardship, but her eyes were kind and filled with a quiet strength.

"Do not lose hope, child," the woman whispered. "We have each other, and we have our memories. They cannot take that from us."

Aminata nodded, tears filling her eyes. "I miss my mother," she whispered back. "I miss my home."

"I know," the woman said gently. "But we must stay strong, for them. We must survive, so that their memory lives on through us."

As the journey continued, Aminata drew strength from the woman's words. She knew that she had to stay strong, not just for herself, but for her mother and for the village that had given her so much. She vowed to survive, to find a way back to her people, and to honor the memory of those they had lost.

The road ahead was uncertain and filled with danger, but Aminata's spirit was unbroken. She faced each day with a fierce determination, her heart filled with the love and strength of her mother. The future was unknown, but Aminata was ready to face whatever challenges lay ahead.

....

BACK IN THE VILLAGE, the survivors began the slow process of rebuilding their lives. The pain of loss was a constant presence, but they found solace in their shared grief and their determination to honor those they had lost. The elders guided them with wisdom and compassion, helping them find a way forward.

The villagers planted new crops, repaired their homes, and cared for each other with a renewed sense of community. The scars of the raid would never fully heal, but they drew strength from their resilience and their bonds of love and friendship.

As they worked to rebuild, the villagers often spoke of Abeni and her unwavering strength. Her legacy lived on through Aminata, whose courage and determination inspired those who knew her. The memory of Abeni's love, wisdom and storytelling skills was a guiding light for the village, a beacon of hope in their darkest times.

Aminata's journey was far from over, but the love and support of her village would always be with her. She carried the lessons of her mother and her community in her heart, facing each new challenge with the strength and resilience they had instilled in her.

The future was uncertain, but Aminata was ready to face it with the same courage and determination that had carried her through the darkest moments of her life. She knew that no matter what lay ahead, she would honor the memory of her mother and her village by never giving up, by staying strong, and by always fighting for the people she loved.

A fter enduring the grueling journey from their village, Aminata and her fellow captives found themselves sold to a buyer who owned a large Arab ship. The reality of their new life as slaves began to sink in as they were herded onto the massive vessel, their wrists still bound and their bodies weak from exhaustion and fear.

The ship was a floating prison, its belly filled with the stench of human misery. The captives were crammed into the ship's hold, a dark and suffocating space with barely enough room to move. The air was thick with the smell of sweat, urine, and vomit, a constant reminder of their dire circumstances. The captives were forced to lie in their own filth, their bodies pressed together so tightly that movement was almost impossible.

The crew of the ship, hardened and ruthless, showed no mercy to the captives. The slavers were men of brutal disposition, their eyes cold and devoid of empathy. They wielded whips with practiced ease, ready to strike at the slightest hint of defiance or weakness. The sound of the whip cracking through the air was a constant, terrifying presence, a reminder of the pain that awaited those who stepped out of line.

The slavers barked orders in a harsh, guttural language that Aminata and the others could barely understand. Their voices were filled with contempt and cruelty, treating the captives as less than human. They laughed and jeered at the sight of their suffering, deriving a perverse pleasure from their pain. The captives were given barely enough food and water to survive, their rations consisting of moldy bread and brackish water that left them more parched than before.

. . . .

THE CONDITIONS IN THE slave chambers were beyond deplorable. The captives were packed so tightly that there was no room to lie down or stretch. Many of them were forced to sit or squat for hours on end, their muscles cramping and their bodies aching from the confinement. The floor of the hold was slick with urine and feces, and the smell was overwhelming. Vomit added to the putrid mix, as the rocking of the ship caused many to succumb to seasickness.

Disease spread rapidly in the cramped, filthy conditions. The captives' bodies were covered in open sores and festering wounds, the result of constant friction and lack of hygiene. Infections were rampant, and without proper medical care, many of the captives succumbed to illness. Fever, dysentery, and respiratory infections took a heavy toll, and the bodies of the dead were callously tossed overboard by the slavers, who showed no concern for their lives.

The mental torture was as relentless as the physical. The captives were stripped of their identities, treated as mere commodities to be bought and sold. They were forced to endure the constant humiliation of being poked and prodded by the slavers, who assessed their worth with a cold, calculating eye. The captives' spirits were crushed under the weight of their hopelessness, their minds battered by the constant fear and uncertainty of their future.

Aminata clung to the memory of her mother, drawing strength from the love and warmth they had shared. She sang songs under her breath, the melodies a lifeline in the sea of despair. The other captives joined her, their voices a mournful chorus that echoed through the hold. The songs were a way to remember who they were, a defiance against the slavers' attempts to strip them of their humanity.

. . . .

THE CAPTIVES' SONGS were filled with sorrow and longing, a reflection of their suffering. They sang of their homes, their families, and the lives they had lost. The melodies were haunting and beautiful, a testament to their resilience and strength. The songs were a way to connect with each other, to find solace in their shared pain. They sang through their tears, their voices trembling with emotion.

"Awa nyi, awa nyi, kedo awo," Aminata sang softly, her voice blending with the others. "Our home, our home, we long for you."

The songs were a source of comfort, but they also brought a deep sense of sadness. The captives cried openly, their tears mingling with the filth on the floor. They clung to each other, finding solace in their shared sorrow. The slavers mocked their tears, but the captives held on to their humanity through their songs and their grief.

The captives' bodies were a testament to the cruelty they endured. Whip marks crisscrossed their backs, the flesh raw and bleeding. The slavers used the whips to maintain control, the threat of pain a constant presence. The wounds festered in the filthy conditions, becoming infected and oozing pus. The captives' skin was covered in sores, the result of constant friction and lack of hygiene.

Aminata's back was a patchwork of scars, the result of countless beatings. The pain was a constant, throbbing presence, but she refused to let it break her spirit. She drew strength from the memory of her mother, her resolve to survive stronger than ever. She knew that she had to stay strong, not just for herself, but for the others who looked to her for strength.

. . . .

THE CAPTIVES WERE TERRIFIED of what lay ahead. The journey across the sea was long and grueling, and the uncertainty of their fate was a constant source of fear. They whispered to each other in the dark, sharing their fears and their hopes. They spoke of their homes, of the lives they had lost, and of the future that awaited them.

"Do you think we will ever see our homes again?" one of the captives asked, his voice trembling with fear.

"I don't know," another replied, "but we must stay strong. We must survive, for our families, for our homes."

Aminata listened to their words, drawing strength from their resolve. She knew that they had to stay strong, that they had to survive whatever lay ahead. The future was uncertain, but she was determined to face it with courage and resilience.

The slavers showed no mercy to the captives. They treated them with contempt and cruelty, their actions driven by greed and a complete disregard for human life. The captives were beaten and whipped, their bodies bruised and broken by the constant abuse. The slavers took pleasure in their suffering, their laughter a cruel reminder of their power.

The captives were given barely enough food and water to survive, their bodies wasting away from hunger and dehydration. The rations were meager and often spoiled, the water brackish and barely drinkable. The captives were forced to drink and eat whatever they were given, their hunger and thirst overriding their revulsion.

. . . .

EACH DAY WAS A STRUGGLE for survival. The captives clung to their humanity, finding strength in their shared suffering and their determination to survive. They drew strength from each other, their bonds growing stronger with each passing day. The journey was long and grueling, but they refused to give up.

Aminata was a beacon of strength for the others. Her resolve to survive, her determination to honor her mother's memory, inspired those around her. She led them in song, her voice a source of comfort and strength. She cared for the others, tending to their wounds as best she could, offering words of encouragement and hope.

The journey across the sea seemed endless. The days and nights blended together, the constant motion of the ship a reminder of their captivity. The captives dreamed of home, of the lives they had lost, but the reality of their situation was a constant, harsh reminder of their fate. They knew that they had to stay strong, that they had to survive whatever lay ahead.

Despite the horrors they endured, the captives held on to a glimmer of hope. They dreamed of a future where they might find freedom, where they might see their homes again. They drew strength from their shared suffering, their bonds of love and friendship a source

of solace and strength.

Aminata knew that their journey was far from over, but she was determined to face whatever lay ahead with courage and resilience. She drew strength from the memory of her mother, from the love and warmth they had shared. She knew that she had to stay strong, not just for herself, but for the others who looked to her for strength.

The future was uncertain, but Aminata was ready to face it with the same courage and determination that had carried her through the darkest moments of her life. She knew that no matter what lay ahead, she would honor the memory of her mother and her village by never giving up, by staying strong, and by always fighting for the people she loved.

A fter what seemed like an eternity at sea, the ship finally docked. Aminata and her fellow captives were dragged onto the shore, their bodies weak and minds weary from the grueling journey. They were in a strange new land, later learning it was called America, a place none of them had ever imagined existed. Everything about this place was foreign to them: the land, the people, the language, and the customs.

The captives were quickly herded into a bustling slave market. The market was chaotic, filled with the shouts of traders and the cries of the captives. Aminata was horrified by what she saw. The slaves were lined up, their bodies inspected and touched in the most humiliating ways by potential buyers.

"Open your mouth!" a rough voice commanded. Aminata flinched as a greasy hand forced her jaws apart, inspecting her teeth as if she were an animal. Her skin crawled as more hands prodded her body, assessing her strength and health. She stood there, exposed and humiliated, feeling every ounce of her dignity stripped away.

"Good strong legs on this one," one buyer commented, his voice dripping with condescension. "She'll fetch a good price."

The buyers were a strange assortment of characters. Some were rotund and sweaty, their wealth displayed in their opulent clothing and arrogant demeanors. Others were skinny and grim, their faces twisted with cruelty. One man in particular had a wild look in his eyes, mumbling to himself as he examined the slaves. His clothes were tattered, and he smelled of alcohol, staggering as he moved from one captive to the next.

Another potential buyer, a woman with a stern face and piercing eyes, inspected the captives with a cold, calculating gaze. She moved with an air of superiority, her presence commanding fear and obedience. She scrutinized every slave she came across, muttering disapprovingly before moving on to the next.

Finally, a massive man with a mean face approached Aminata. His eyes were small and dark, set deep in a face that rarely smiled. His presence was intimidating, and he exuded an aura of authority and menace. He was dressed in expensive clothing, but his demeanor was far from refined.

"This one," he grunted, pointing at Aminata. "Load her onto the cart."

· · · ·

AMINATA WAS QUICKLY bound and loaded onto a cart, joining several other newly purchased slaves. As the cart rumbled through the streets, she was astonished by the sights around her. She saw lots of people with white skin, something she had never encountered before.

Their faces were strange to her, their mannerisms foreign and unsettling.

The buildings were unlike anything she had ever seen. They were made of rock and concrete, towering over the bustling streets. The noise was overwhelming: the clatter of hooves on cobblestone, the shouts of vendors, and the constant hum of activity. Aminata's senses were overwhelmed by the strangeness of it all.

"Look at that," she whispered to a fellow captive, pointing to a strange vehicle moving without any animals pulling it. "What is that?"

"I don't know," the other replied, equally bewildered. "Everything here is so strange."

As the cart left the town and moved into the countryside, Aminata saw vast fields stretching out on either side of the road. The fields were filled with slaves working under the harsh supervision of overseers. Some were picking cotton, their fingers moving quickly through the plants. Others were chopping wood or tending to livestock. The overseers carried whips, and the sound of cracking leather was a constant backdrop to their labor.

Aminata's heart sank as she watched a slave being whipped for not working fast enough. The overseer's face was twisted in anger as he lashed the man's back, leaving deep, bloody welts. The slave's cries of pain echoed in the air, mingling with the sounds of nature.

"Move faster, you worthless dog!" the overseer shouted. "You'll get twice the lashes if you don't keep up!"

As they continued their journey, Aminata suddenly saw a slave running desperately towards their cart. His face was a mask of terror, his breath coming in ragged gasps. He stumbled and fell, his body scraping against the rough ground. But he quickly got up and continued running, his eyes wide with fear.

"Help me!" he cried, his voice hoarse. "Please, help me!"

In hot pursuit were four men on horses, accompanied by snarling dogs. The riders spurred their horses forward, shouting commands and encouragement to the dogs. The runner slave's face was a picture of desperation as he tried to escape, his body moving with frantic energy.

"Stop him!" one of the riders yelled. "Don't let him get away!"

The slave managed to reach the side of the cart, grabbing onto it for support. Aminata watched in horror as the riders closed in. One of the dogs leapt at the runner, its jaws snapping shut on his leg. The man screamed in pain, trying to shake the dog off, but it held on with relentless determination.

"Please, let me go!" the runner pleaded, tears streaming down his face. "I just want to be free!"

The runners' desperate bid for freedom ended in vain. The riders pulled him off the cart, beating him mercilessly before tying him up and dragging him behind their horses. Aminata could only watch, her heart breaking for the man who had come so close to escaping only to be recaptured.

The   cart continued its journey, taking Aminata further into a world of unimaginable cruelty and suffering. She felt a deep sense of dread as they approached her new home, knowing that her life would never be the same. The memories of her village, her mother, and the life she had once known seemed like distant dreams.

When the cart finally stopped, Aminata was roughly pulled down and led to her new master's home. The plantation was vast, with fields stretching as far as the eye could see. Slaves worked tirelessly under the watchful eyes of overseers, their bodies bent with exhaustion.

The huge buyer with the mean face, who had bought Aminata at the market, approached her with a smirk. "Welcome to your new home," he said, his voice dripping with mockery. "You belong to me now. You will work hard, and if you disobey, you will be punished. Do you understand?"

She could hardly understand what he was saying. Aminata nodded, her heart heavy with despair. She knew that her life would be filled with hardship and suffering, but she resolved to stay strong. She thought of her mother's strength and courage, drawing inspiration from her memory.

. . . .

AS AMINATA WAS BEING led to her quarters that evening, she witnessed the brutal reality of plantation life. Slaves were whipped for the slightest infraction, their bodies bearing the scars of constant abuse. The overseers were relentless, their cruelty knowing no bounds. The slaves' faces were etched with pain and hopelessness, their spirits broken by years of relentless labor and punishment.

Aminata was lead to the slave quarters were small and cramped structures, with barely enough room to lie down were. The air was thick with the smell of sweat and despair. She was led to a dilapidated building that seemed on the verge of collapse. The walls were made of rough, untreated wood, and the roof leaked whenever it rained. The only light came from a few small, grimy windows high up on the walls.

As she entered, Aminata was struck by the silence that hung heavy in the air. The slaves were too exhausted to talk, their eyes hollow and devoid of hope. They moved about like shadows, their bodies bent and broken by years of relentless labor. The weariness on their faces spoke volumes, each line and scar a testament to their suffering.

One figure stood out among the others—a tall, dark man with a muscular frame and a whip hanging from his belt. His presence was intimidating, and he carried himself with an air of authority that was impossible to ignore. Aminata was shocked to see that a fellow black man could wield such power over his own people.

"Who is that?" she whispered to a fellow slave.

"That's Bayo," came the hushed reply. "He's the overseer. We call him the 'Small King.'"

. . . .

BAYO'S REPUTATION PRECEDED him. He was known for his ruthless efficiency and unrelenting cruelty. The other slaves feared him, and with good reason. He enforced the master's will with zeal, often going above and beyond what was required. Bayo seemed to take a perverse pleasure in his role, his whip cracking with terrifying regularity.

Aminata watched in horror as Bayo barked orders and lashed out at anyone who moved too slowly. He was a man of few words, but his actions spoke volumes. The other slaves scurried to obey him, their eyes cast downward in submission.

Aminata's introduction to the quarters was brief and devoid of ceremony. One of the older women, her face etched with years of hardship, handed her a bundle of old rags.

"Here, take these," she said, her voice barely above a whisper. "It's all we have."

Aminata accepted the rags gratefully, though they were little more than scraps of cloth. She looked around, trying to find a place to sleep, but no one offered her any guidance. The floor was covered in straw and dirt, and the air was thick with the stench of unwashed bodies.

As night fell, Aminata found a small corner where she could curl up. The hard floor offered no comfort, and the constant ache in her body made it difficult to find rest. The sounds of the night were filled with the muffled sobs and quiet murmurs of her fellow slaves, each one lost in their own world of pain and despair.

"Try to sleep," the old woman whispered, her voice a soothing balm in the darkness. "Tomorrow will be another hard day."

Aminata closed her eyes, willing herself to sleep. She thought of her mother, of the life she had once known, and a tear slipped down her cheek. She had to survive, for her mother's memory and for the hope of a better future.

Aminata's first night in her new quarters was one of the longest and most restless she had ever experienced. The room was cramped, filled with the quiet murmurs of the other slaves. The hard floor offered no comfort, and the thin rags that served as her bedding did little to protect her from the cold. Exhaustion finally overtook her, and she drifted into a fitful sleep.

In her dream, she found herself back in her village. The sun was rising, casting a golden glow over the lush landscape. She could hear the cheerful chatter of the villagers, the laughter of children playing, and the soothing sounds of nature all around. Her mother, Abeni, was there, her face glowing with happiness as she tended to the garden.

Aminata walked through the village, breathing in the fresh air, her heart swelling with joy. She reached out to touch the vibrant flowers, feeling their soft petals beneath her fingers. It was a perfect moment, a slice of the paradise she had lost. She closed her eyes, letting the warmth of the sun wash over her.

But then, out of nowhere, a furious bull charged at her. Its eyes were wild, and its horns gleamed menacingly in the sunlight. Aminata tried to move, but her feet felt rooted to the ground. The bull came closer and closer until it was right upon her. Just as it was about to strike, she felt a sharp pain in her side, and she woke up with a start.

Standing over her was Bayo, his face twisted in anger. He had kicked her awake, his boot still pressed against her ribs.

"Wake up, you don't have all day!" he shouted, his voice echoing in the dark room.

Aminata scrambled to her feet, her heart pounding. She was not at home. The comforting sights and sounds of her village were gone, replaced by the harsh reality of her new life. The other slaves stirred around her, their eyes avoiding hers as they prepared for another grueling day of labor.

Bayo continued to bark orders, his whip cracking in the air to emphasize his commands. "Get up, all of you! Move faster! We have work to do!"

Aminata and the others quickly gathered outside, where they were given meager portions of food to sustain them through the day's work. The sky was still dark, the stars barely visible against the inky blackness. The cool morning air bit at their exposed skin, but there was no time to linger.

The slaves moved in a silent procession to the fields, their footsteps heavy with fatigue. Aminata's muscles ached from the previous day's struggles, but she forced herself to keep going. She knew that any sign of weakness would invite Bayo's wrath.

THE WORK IN THE FIELDS was backbreaking. They were tasked with picking cotton, a job that required nimble fingers and a strong back. The plants were covered in sharp thorns that tore at their skin, leaving bloody scratches. The sun had not yet risen, but already the promise of another scorching day hung in the air.

Aminata worked alongside her fellow slaves, her hands moving mechanically. She tried to focus on the task at hand, but her mind kept drifting back to her dream. The image of her mother, so happy and alive, was a stark contrast to the reality she faced now.

Bayo patrolled the fields, his eyes scanning for any sign of slacking. He took a perverse pleasure in his role, his whip a constant reminder of the consequences of disobedience.

"You there!" he shouted, pointing his whip at a young girl who had paused to rest for a moment. "Move faster, or I'll give you something to cry about!"

The girl, no older than twelve, scrambled to comply, her eyes wide with fear. Bayo's whip cracked in the air, a warning to all who might think of slowing down. Aminata's heart ached for the girl, but she knew there was nothing she could do. Any attempt to intervene would only bring more suffering.

The hours dragged on, each one blending into the next. The sun climbed higher in the sky, its heat becoming almost unbearable. Sweat poured down Aminata's face, stinging her eyes and making her hands slick. The work seemed endless, and every part of her body screamed in protest.

By midday, Aminata was on the verge of collapse. Her vision blurred, and she stumbled over her own feet. But Bayo was there, his whip a constant threat, and she forced herself to keep moving.

"Faster! We don't have all day!" Bayo's voice was a relentless drumbeat, driving them forward.

At last, they were given a brief respite to eat and drink. The slaves gathered under the sparse shade of a tree, their movements slow and exhausted. Aminata sat down heavily, her body trembling with fatigue. She took a few bites of the coarse bread and sipped the tepid water, her stomach churning with hunger and nausea.

Asha, the older woman who had given her the rags, sat beside her. "You did well today," she said quietly, her voice filled with sympathy. "It's not easy, but you must stay strong."

Aminata nodded, too tired to speak. She closed her eyes for a moment, trying to gather her strength for the second half of the day.

• • • •

THE AFTERNOON WAS EVEN more grueling than the morning. The sun was at its peak, beating down on them mercilessly. Aminata's hands were raw and bleeding, her back ached, and her head throbbed with pain. But she kept going, driven by a fierce determination to survive.

Bayo continued to patrol, his whip cracking in the air like a gunshot. "Keep moving! No rest for the weak!"

Aminata's vision blurred again, and she stumbled, nearly falling. Bayo was there in an instant, his whip lashing out at her back. She bit back a cry of pain, forcing herself to stand upright.

"You're not done yet," he snarled. "Get back to work."

As the sun began to set, the slaves were finally allowed to stop. They trudged back to the quarters, their bodies aching and their spirits crushed. Aminata collapsed onto the hard floor, too exhausted to even think about eating. She closed her eyes, but sleep was elusive, her mind replaying the horrors of the day.

That night, Aminata dreamed again. She was back in her village, the sun setting in a blaze of color. Her mother was there, her face serene and happy. They were sitting by the river, the water sparkling in the fading light.

"It's beautiful, isn't it?" Abeni said, her voice filled with warmth.

"Yes, it is," Aminata replied, her heart aching with longing.

But then, the sky darkened, and a storm began to brew. The river swelled, and a torrent of water rushed towards them. Aminata tried to hold onto her mother, but the current was too strong. She was swept away, her mother's face disappearing into the darkness.

Aminata woke with a start, her heart pounding. Bayo was standing over her again, his boot nudging her side.

"Wake up, you lazy dog! You don't have all day!"

It was still dark outside, and Aminata's body ached with fatigue. She dragged herself to her feet, the weight of her new reality pressing down on her. She glanced around at the other slaves, their faces filled with the same exhaustion and despair.

The days blended into one another, each one a repetition of the last. The work was relentless, the conditions unbearable. Aminata's body became a patchwork of bruises and scars, each one a testament to her struggle for survival. But through it all, she held onto a glimmer of hope, a tiny spark that kept her going.

Asha's words echoed in her mind. "Stay strong. They can break our bodies, but not our spirits."

Aminata vowed to survive, to honor her mother's memory, and to one day find freedom again. The journey was far from over, but she faced each new day with courage and determination, refusing to let the cruelty of her captors extinguish her spirit.

As the days turned into weeks, Aminata adapted to her new life on the plantation. She found solace in the small acts of kindness from her fellow slaves, who shared their food and offered words of encouragement. They sang songs in the fields, their voices a reminder of their shared humanity and resilience.

Aminata's spirit remained unbroken, despite the constant hardships. She held on to the hope that one day, she might find freedom again. The journey was far from over, but Aminata was determined to face whatever lay ahead with courage and strength. She knew that her mother's legacy lived on in her, and that she would honor her memory by never giving up.

As the days turned into weeks, Aminata adapted to her new life on the plantation. The rhythm of the days became familiar, and she found small moments of solace amid the relentless labor. Her fellow slaves, though weary and worn, were a source of strength and resilience. They shared their meager food rations, offered words of encouragement, and, most importantly, sang songs that lifted their spirits and connected them to their shared humanity.

In the fields, under the scorching sun, the slaves sang songs that told their stories, expressed their sorrows, and nurtured their hopes. The songs were a blend of African rhythms and melodies, interwoven with the pain and resilience of their current lives. Aminata learned these songs quickly, feeling the power of their words and the comfort of their familiar tunes.

One song, in particular, resonated deeply with Aminata. It was a song about freedom, a distant dream that still lived in the hearts of the slaves.

Freedom Song
Oh, freedom, oh, freedom, oh, freedom over me
And before I'll be a slave, I'll be buried in my grave

And go home to my Lord and be free
No more weepin', no more weepin', no more weepin' over me
And before I'll be a slave, I'll be buried in my grave
And go home to my Lord and be free

The chorus echoed through the fields, a haunting reminder of the lives they once knew and the hope that still burned within them.

• • • •

IN THE EVENINGS, AFTER the long hours of toil, the slaves would gather and share stories. These stories were a mix of memories from their homelands, tales of resistance, and accounts of the brutal realities they faced.

One of the elders, Papa Jomo, often told the story of a slave named Kunta who had attempted to escape. The story was a cautionary tale but also a testament to the indomitable spirit of those who refused to be broken.

"Y'all know Kunta," Papa Jomo would begin, his voice a low rumble. "He was strong, real strong. One night, he decided he couldn't take it no more. He ran through them woods like a deer, fast and quiet."

The slaves would lean in closer, the flickering light of the fire casting shadows on their faces.

"But they caught him," Papa Jomo continued, his voice heavy with sorrow. "Caught him and made an example outta him. Burned him at the stake for all to see. But Kunta, he didn't cry out. He faced 'em with courage, showed 'em he was more than just a slave."

Despite the constant threat of punishment, whispers of revolt and resistance were never far from the slaves' conversations. Stories circulated of slaves who had managed to kill their masters, of daring escapes, and of small acts of defiance.

Aminata heard tales of slaves spitting in their masters' food, lacing it with feces, and finding other ways to mete out small punishments.

These acts, though seemingly minor, were powerful statements of their refusal to be completely subjugated.

"Did ya hear 'bout Big Joe?" one slave whispered to Aminata. "He spat in Massa's soup. Massa ate it up, none the wiser."

Aminata couldn't help but smile at the thought. Even in the face of such cruelty, they found ways to fight back, to maintain a shred of dignity and defiance.

Occasionally, the slaves were allowed brief moments of reprieve, small pleasures that provided a glimmer of hope. They were permitted to hold a modest party or a gathering where they could sing, dance, and forget their woes for a short while.

During these gatherings, there was often preaching. A fellow slave, known as Preacher Sam, would hold a worn Bible as he spoke to the group. Aminata noticed that he never opened the book, which puzzled her.

One night, she asked a fellow slave, a young woman named Nia, about it. "Why Preacher Sam never open dat book? What he holdin' it for?"

Nia looked at her with a mix of surprise and amusement. "He don't know how to read," she explained. "Dat book jus' for show. He teachin' us what he was told by the white folks."

Aminata frowned. "But how we know what he teachin' is true if he can't read it for hisself?"

Nia shrugged. "We don't know. We jus' listen and hope he speakin' the truth."

As time passed, Aminata began to pick up the language spoken by the other slaves. It was a dialect different from the English of their masters, rich with African influences and new words. They called it Black American English.

"Dis language, it's somethin' else," Aminata thought. "A mix of all we been through, all we lost, and all we hold on to."

She marveled at how the slaves had created a way of speaking that was uniquely theirs, a testament to their resilience and adaptability. The language was a means of survival, a way to communicate and bond in the face of oppression.

• • • •

ONE SUNDAY, DURING a rare moment of rest, Aminata approached Preacher Sam. She had been thinking about their conversations and had more questions.

"Preacher Sam," she began hesitantly, "why you hold dat book if you can't read it?"

Preacher Sam looked at her, a flicker of sadness in his eyes. "Chile, I hold it 'cause it give folks hope. Dey see it and dey believe in somethin' bigger than dis life. It's a symbol."

"But how you know what you preachin' is true?" Aminata pressed.

Preacher Sam sighed. "I don't know, not for sure. But I speak from my heart, and I hope dat's enough. We all need somethin' to believe in, Aminata. Somethin' to keep us goin'."

Aminata nodded, understanding the weight of his words. Even in their darkest moments, they needed hope, something to hold on to.

Despite the constant hardships, Aminata's spirit remained unbroken. She drew strength from the stories, songs, and the small acts of defiance that defined their lives. She knew that her mother's legacy lived on in her, and she was determined to honor her memory by never giving up.

She also found a new resolve growing within her. The whispers of revolt, the stories of resistance, and the small pleasures they shared fueled her determination. She realized that surviving was not enough; she needed to live with purpose, to find a way to fight back, even in small ways.

The cruelty of the slave masters was a constant presence. They were men who reveled in their power, who saw the slaves as mere property to be exploited. Aminata witnessed their brutality firsthand, but she also saw glimpses of their weaknesses.

One master, in particular, was known for his cruelty. He was a tall, imposing man with a permanent scowl etched on his face. He took pleasure in the suffering of the slaves, using his whip with a savage delight.

But even he was not immune to the small acts of resistance. Aminata heard whispers of how some slaves had found ways to make his life difficult, poisoning his food with laxatives, sabotaging his equipment, killing his animals and finding other ways to fight back.

* * * *

ONE EVENING, THE SLAVES were allowed a brief respite to hold a small party. It was a rare occasion, and they made the most of it. They sang, danced, and shared stories, finding joy in each other's company.

Aminata marveled at their resilience. Despite everything they had endured, they still found ways to celebrate, to hold on to their humanity.

Preacher Sam held his usual sermon, the worn Bible in his hands. He spoke with passion, his voice rising and falling in a rhythm that captivated his listeners.

"We are children of God," he proclaimed. "And no matter what dey do to us, dey can't take away our souls. We must stay strong, stay together, and hold on to our faith."

Aminata listened, feeling a sense of hope and determination growing within her. She knew that their journey was far from over, but she was ready to face whatever lay ahead with courage and strength.

* * * *

AS AMINATA LEARNED more of the Black American English, she began to understand its power. It was a language born of their shared experiences, a way to communicate and bond in the face of oppression.

She practiced speaking it, listening to the cadences and rhythms of her fellow slaves. It was a language that spoke of resilience, of survival, and of hope.

With each passing day, Aminata's resolve grew stronger. She was determined to honor her mother's memory, to survive and find a way to fight back. She knew that their journey was far from over, but she was ready to face whatever lay ahead with courage and strength.

In the midst of their suffering, they found ways to resist, to hold on to their humanity, and to support each other. They were more than just slaves; they were survivors, warriors, and symbols of resilience.

Aminata knew that she was not alone. She had her fellow slaves, their songs, their stories, and their shared language. Together, they would endure, and together, they would find a way to fight for their freedom.

Years passed, and Aminata grew into a stunningly beautiful woman. Despite her ragged clothes and the grime of the fields, her beauty was undeniable. Her eyes, still filled with the spirit of her homeland, shone brightly against her dark skin, and her posture, even after years of hard labor, was proud and graceful.

One day, the plantation owner, Mr. Thompson, who often visited the fields to inspect the work, noticed Aminata. He was a man in his early forties, with a stern face and a cold demeanor. His eyes lingered on Aminata longer than usual, and he made a decision.

"You, girl," he called out, pointing directly at her. "Come with me."

Aminata, confused and wary, followed him. She had heard stories about slaves being taken to work in the big house, and while it was seen as a promotion of sorts, it also came with its own set of dangers.

• • • •

THE THOMPSON MANSION was grand and imposing, a stark contrast to the dilapidated quarters of the slaves. The house was built of stone and wood, with large windows and finely crafted doors. Inside, the floors were polished to a gleaming shine, and the furniture was ornate and expensive.

Mrs. Thompson, a woman in her late thirties with a sharp tongue and a cruel streak, was waiting at the door. She was accompanied by her two children: James, a boy of ten, and Mary, a girl of eight. Both children had inherited their mother's cruelty and their father's disdain for the slaves.

"Who is this?" Mrs. Thompson asked sharply, her eyes narrowing as she looked at Aminata.

"This is the new housemaid," Mr. Thompson replied, his tone dismissive. "She will work in the house from now on."

Mrs. Thompson eyed Aminata with suspicion and disdain. "Very well," she said curtly. "Get her to work immediately."

· · · ·

LIFE IN THE THOMPSON mansion was anything but easy. Aminata quickly learned that Mrs. Thompson was a demanding and harsh taskmaster. She was never satisfied, always finding fault with Aminata's work. The children were no better. James and Mary delighted in causing trouble and blaming the slaves for their own misdeeds.

One morning, James, with his mischievous grin, deliberately knocked over a tray of expensive porcelain dishes, shattering them on the floor.

"Mama! Mama!" he cried out, tears welling up in his eyes. "Aminata broke the dishes!"

Mrs. Thompson stormed into the room, her face a mask of fury. "Aminata!" she screamed. "How dare you break my fine China!"

Aminata, standing in the corner, tried to protest. "Ma'am, I didn't—"

"Silence!" Mrs. Thompson cut her off, grabbing a whip from the wall. "You will learn your place."

The sting of the whip was something Aminata had grown used to, but it never hurt any less. Mrs. Thompson lashed out with fury, each strike a reminder of Aminata's helplessness.

Later that night, in the slaves' quarters, Aminata's back bore fresh wounds. The other slaves, weary and silent, looked at her with sympathy but could do little to help.

· · · ·

AMINATA NOTICED THAT Mr. Thompson's eyes followed her whenever she was in the room. His gaze made her uncomfortable, and she did her best to avoid him. However, Mrs. Thompson was quick to notice her husband's interest.

"Why do you keep looking at that girl?" she demanded one evening, her voice filled with venom.

Mr. Thompson spat with contempt. "Don't be ridiculous, woman. She's just a monkey, a dirty filth nonhuman creature."

But Mrs. Thompson was not convinced. Her hatred for Aminata grew, fueled by jealousy and suspicion.

The children continued to make life difficult for Aminata and the other housemaids. One afternoon, Mary spilled ink all over the dining table and then pointed at Aminata.

"She did it, Mama! She made the mess!"

Mrs. Thompson, already on edge, didn't hesitate. "You clumsy fool!" she screamed at Aminata. "You will clean this up and then you'll be punished!"

Then one evening, as Aminata was cleaning the kitchen, James deliberately knocked a bowl of flour onto the floor. "Aminata did it!" he yelled, running to his mother.

Mrs. Thompson, her face red with anger, grabbed Aminata by the arm. "I will not tolerate this incompetence!" she shouted.

"But I didn't—" Aminata began, but the slap that followed silenced her.

"Get out of my sight," Mrs. Thompson hissed. "You will clean every inch of this kitchen until it shines, and then you will be whipped."

As the days went on, Aminata learned to endure the constant punishments and insults. She found small moments of solace in the kindness of the other slaves, who shared their food and offered words of encouragement.

One evening, after a particularly harsh beating, Aminata sat in the slaves' quarters, tears streaming down her face. An older slave, Mama June, sat down beside her.

"Child, you gotta be strong," Mama June said softly. "Dis life ain't easy, but you gotta hold on to hope."

Aminata nodded, wiping her tears. "Thank you, Mama June."

• • • •

LIFE IN THE THOMPSON mansion was a constant struggle. The family's cruelty knew no bounds, and the punishments were relentless. The slaves were treated like animals, forced to work long hours with little rest. The children, James and Mary, were especially cruel, often finding ways to get the slaves into trouble.

One day, James decided to play a particularly cruel prank. He spilled a bucket of water on the kitchen floor and then ran to his mother.

"Mama, Aminata spilled the water!" he cried.

Mrs. Thompson, already in a foul mood, stormed into the kitchen. "Aminata!" she shouted. "How dare you make such a mess!"

"But ma'am, I didn't—" Aminata began, but the slap across her face silenced her.

"You will clean this up immediately, and then you will be whipped," Mrs. Thompson hissed.

Aminata's troubles were compounded by Mr. Thompson's increasing interest in her. His eyes followed her whenever she was in the room, and he found excuses to be near her. Mrs. Thompson noticed and confronted him on several occasions.

"Why do you keep looking at that girl?" she demanded one evening again.

Mr. Thompson responded with contempt. "Don't be ridiculous, woman. She's just a monkey, a dirty filth nonhuman creature."

But Mrs. Thompson was not convinced again.

• • • •

IN THE EVENINGS, THE slaves would gather in their quarters, sharing stories and offering each other comfort. They spoke in hushed tones, their voices filled with weariness but also a resolve to survive.

"Aminata, you gotta keep yo' head up," said an older woman named Nia. "Dis ain't easy, but we gotta stick together."

"I know," Aminata replied. "But it's so hard sometimes."

"We all know dat," Nia said. 'But we gotta hold on to hope. One day, maybe, we'll be free."

The air was crisp with the chill of winter as the Thompson plantation buzzed with activity. It was Christmas, and the Thompsons were hosting a grand celebration. Aminata and the other house slaves worked tirelessly to prepare the mansion for the arrival of guests. Every corner had to be spotless, every piece of silver polished to a gleaming shine. The aroma of roasted meats and freshly baked pies wafted through the halls, mingling with the scent of pine from the towering Christmas tree adorned with candles and handmade ornaments.

As the sun dipped below the horizon, the guests began to arrive. They were a colorful assortment of the local gentry, each more pompous and ostentatious than the last. The men wore fine coats and hats, their wives draped in silks and satins. Their faces were flushed with the anticipation of a night of indulgence.

There was Mr. Jefferson, a rotund man with a booming laugh and a penchant for cigars. His wife, a delicate woman with a perpetually disapproving expression, clung to his arm like a fragile ornament. Mr. Sinclair, a tall, thin man with a monocle and an air of superiority, arrived with his wife, a loud and boisterous woman who dominated every conversation.

Among the guests was a man named Mr. Henderson, a wealthy landowner known for his cruelty. His slaves spoke of him in hushed tones, their voices trembling with fear. He had a keen eye for beauty and power, and tonight, his gaze would fall upon Aminata.

Aminata moved through the crowd, serving drinks and avoiding the leering stares of the guests. She had grown used to being invisible, but tonight, she felt particularly exposed. Her beauty, which had once been her shield, now seemed to draw unwanted attention.

"Who is that girl?" Mr. Henderson asked, his voice dripping with curiosity.

"Her?" Mr. Thompson replied, his eyes narrowing. "That's Aminata. She's one of our housemaids."

Mr. Henderson's eyes lingered on Aminata, a predatory gleam in his gaze. "She's quite a beauty," he said, a twisted smile curling his lips. "I'd like to make an offer for her."

Mr. Thompson's face darkened. "Aminata is not for sale," he said coldly. "She is a valuable worker here."

Mr. Henderson chuckled. "Every slave has a price, Thompson. Name yours."

Mr. Thompson's anger flared. "I said she's not for sale. Now drop it."

• • • •

THE GUESTS MINGLED, their laughter and chatter filling the room. They represented a variety of professions: wealthy landowners, merchants, bankers, and a few local politicians. Each had their own way of treating their slaves, but most shared a common disdain for them.

Mr. Jefferson, for instance, prided himself on his collection of slaves. He treated them as mere commodities, interchangeable and disposable. "Slaves are like cattle," he often said. "Keep them fed and working, and they'll serve you well."

Mr. Sinclair, on the other hand, saw his slaves as extensions of his wealth and status. He dressed them well and paraded them in front of guests, but any disobedience was met with severe punishment. "A well-dressed slave reflects a well-run household," he would say, puffing on his cigar.

As the evening progressed, the conversation turned to one particular master, Mr. Williams, who was known for treating his slaves with an unusual degree of kindness. He even gave them a shilling each year as a token of appreciation.

"Did you hear about Williams?" Mr. Jefferson sneered. "He gives his slaves a shilling every year. What a fool!"

The other guests laughed, their voices filled with contempt.

"A slave is a slave," Mr. Sinclair said, shaking his head. "Treat them with contempt, and they'll respect you. Torture them to near death, and they'll worship you."

"Exactly," Mr. Henderson chimed in. "They'll love you so much they'll kill their fellow brothers for you."

As Aminata served drinks, she overheard the conversations, her heart heavy with the knowledge of the cruelty that surrounded her. She moved through the room like a shadow, trying to avoid the prying eyes of the guests, especially Mr. Henderson's.

In the kitchen, the maids exchanged glances of understanding and fear. They knew the dangers of a night like this, where the boundaries of decency were often blurred by alcohol and arrogance.

As the evening wore on, young James, the Thompson boy, decided to entertain himself at Aminata's expense. He sneaked into the dining room, where Aminata was setting the table, and deliberately knocked over a tray of utensils, causing a loud crash.

"Mama! Mama!" he screamed, tears streaming down his face. "Aminata broke the utensils!"

Mrs. Thompson stormed in, her face a mask of rage. "Aminata!" she shouted. "How dare you break my fine silver!"

"But ma'am, I didn't—" Aminata began, but Mrs. Thompson silenced her with a slap.

"You clumsy fool!" she screamed. "You will be whipped for this!"

Mr. Thompson, already irritated by Mr. Henderson's earlier proposal, took out his anger on Aminata. She was dragged out to the yard, and the guests gathered to watch, their faces twisted with cruel anticipation.

As the whip cracked across her back, Aminata bit her lip to keep from crying out. Each lash was a searing reminder of her powerlessness, but also of her determination to survive.

That night, as Aminata lay in her small, cramped quarters, her back burning with pain, she thought about the day's events. The other slaves offered her quiet words of comfort, their eyes filled with understanding.

"We gonna get through this," Mama June whispered, her voice steady. "We gotta stay strong."

Aminata nodded her resolve hardening. She thought of her mother and the strength she had inherited from her. She would survive, no matter what.

The sun had barely set when Mr. Thompson stumbled through the door, reeking of alcohol. His wife, Mrs. Thompson, had gone to see the doctor with the children and one of the maids. The household was eerily quiet, the absence of Mrs. Thompson's sharp tongue and the children's mischief a stark contrast to the usual chaos.

Aminata, lost in her chores, tried to ignore the sinking feeling in her stomach. She had learned to anticipate trouble, and today, the air was thick with it. She continued to scrub the floor, hoping to remain invisible.

Mr. Thompson wandered around the house, his eyes bloodshot and glazed. He spotted Aminata and lingered, his gaze becoming more sinister with each passing moment. He stumbled towards the garage, where old tools and hunting gear were kept, and shouted for a young slave boy nearby.

"Hey, boy! Go fetch Aminata. Tell her to come to the garage," he slurred.

The boy, only eight years old and trembling with fear, approached Aminata. "Miss Aminata, sir wants you in the garage," he whispered, his voice barely audible.

Aminata's heart sank. She looked into the boy's frightened eyes and saw her own fear reflected back. "Thank you, child," she said softly, patting his head. She put down her cleaning rag, wiped her hands on her apron, and made her way to the garage.

The garage was dimly lit, the flickering lantern casting long, ominous shadows. Mr. Thompson stood near the back, leaning against a workbench cluttered with tools and hunting gear.

"Aminata," he called out as she entered, his voice dripping with false sweetness. "I want you to clean and arrange these items here. Make it spotless."

"Yes, sir," Aminata replied, her voice steady but her heart racing. She hesitated for a moment, then began to tidy the workbench.

Mr. Thompson's heavy breathing filled the room as he watched her. She could feel his eyes on her, the weight of his gaze making her skin crawl. Suddenly, he moved closer, his steps unsteady but purposeful.

"You're quite a beauty, Aminata," he said, his voice low and menacing. "It's a shame to waste it."

Aminata's hands trembled as she continued her work, trying to ignore him. But he was relentless. He grabbed her arm, spinning her around to face him. His breath was hot and foul against her cheek.

"No, please," Aminata whispered, trying to pull away.

He slapped her hard, sending her crashing against the workbench. "You don't tell me no," he snarled. He hit her again, this time with his fist, and she tasted blood in her mouth.

Aminata's vision blurred as she tried to steady herself. Mr. Thompson's size and strength overwhelmed her. He ripped at her clothes, his hands rough and unyielding. She screamed, a sound filled with pain and desperation, but there was no one to help.

The other slaves heard her cries, their hearts breaking, but they were powerless. They knew all too well the consequences of intervening. They could only listen, their own tears mingling with her screams.

The assault was brutal. Mr. Thompson's weight pinned her down, his lust and rage overpowering any sense of humanity. Aminata felt her spirit being crushed along with her body. This was her first experience with a man, and it was a nightmare of unimaginable horror.

When it was over, Mr. Thompson staggered to his feet, leaving her bleeding and broken on the cold floor. He adjusted his clothes, muttering curses under his breath, and stumbled back into the house.

• • • •

MRS. THOMPSON RETURNED almost immediately and bumped on her husband rushing from the garage. She peeped inside and spotted Aminata crying. Her face was a mask of fury as she stormed into the garage.

"Aminata!" she screamed. "You filthy seductress! How dare you tempt my husband!"

Aminata, still reeling from the attack, tried to explain. "Ma'am, I didn't—"

"Silence!" Mrs. Thompson shrieked. She grabbed a whip and dragged Aminata outside. The other slaves watched in horror, their hearts heavy with sorrow and helplessness.

Mrs. Thompson's rage was unrestrained. She lashed out at Aminata with the whip, each strike leaving a mark on her already bruised body. "You will learn your place!" she screamed, her voice hoarse with anger.

When Mrs. Thompson grew tired, she called for Bayo, the black overseer. He approached with reluctance, knowing the grim task he was about to perform.

"Continue," Mrs. Thompson ordered, her eyes blazing. "Make sure she understands her place."

Bayo raised the whip, his face expressionless, and continued the punishment. Each crack of the whip echoed in the night, a haunting reminder of the cruelty that ruled their lives. Aminata's screams eventually gave way to silence, her body too exhausted to produce any more sound.

The other slaves watched, their own pain mirrored in Aminata's suffering. Tears streamed down their faces, but they could do nothing. The plantation was silent, even the animals seemed to mourn.

After what felt like an eternity, Mr. Thompson finally emerged from the house. He looked at the scene with a mix of contempt and guilt. "Stop," he ordered Bayo. "We don't want her dead. She's valuable. I bought her with my hard-earned cash, remember?"

Bayo lowered the whip, his relief palpable. He stepped back, leaving Aminata on the ground, her body a tapestry of wounds.

Mr. Thompson turned to the other slaves. "Get her cleaned up," he said coldly. "And get back to work!"

The days that followed were a blur of pain and humiliation for Aminata. The other slaves tended to her wounds as best they could, offering what little comfort they had. Mama June sat by her side, whispering words of hope and strength.

"We gon' get through this, child," she said softly. "You strong. You gon' make it."

Aminata nodded weakly, her spirit still unbroken despite the horrors she had endured. She knew she had to survive, not just for herself, but for the memory of her mother and the hope of a better future.

Even in the darkest times, Aminata found small moments of solace. The other slaves shared stories and songs, their voices a testament to their resilience. They spoke of freedom and justice, whispering about the possibility of escape.

"We gon' make it outta here one day," Isaac said one evening, his voice filled with determination. "We just gotta hold on."

Aminata listened, her heart lifting slightly. She knew the road ahead would be difficult, but she was ready to face whatever lay ahead with courage and strength.

As the months passed, Aminata's resolve only grew stronger. She learned to navigate the treacherous waters of the plantation, finding small ways to resist and assert her dignity. She knew that her journey was far from over, but she was determined to honor her mother's legacy by never giving up.

With each passing day, Aminata's spirit burned brighter, a beacon of hope in a world filled with darkness. She knew that one day, she would find freedom and justice, and she would fight with every ounce of strength she had to achieve it.

· · · ·

THE DAWN OF A NEW DAY brought with it an unexpected twist in Aminata's already tumultuous life. She awoke feeling strangely unsettled, a persistent queasiness in her stomach. As she went about her chores, the feeling intensified.

It was while she was serving tea to the Thompson family that the realization hit her. She was arranging the cups when a sudden wave of nausea overtook her. The room spun, and she felt the bile rising. Hastily placing the tray on the floor, she bolted out of the room, her hand covering her mouth.

Outside, she leaned against the wall, breathing heavily. Bayo, the black overseer, had seen her rush out and followed her. His stern expression softened as he watched her retch into the bushes.

"You pregnant, ain't you?" he asked, his voice low but firm.

Aminata wiped her mouth and looked up at him, her eyes wide with fear and confusion. "I... I don't know," she stammered, though deep down, she knew he was right.

Bayo shook his head, a mixture of pity and frustration in his eyes. "It's obvious who the father is. This ain't good, Aminata."

• • • •

THE NEWS SPREAD QUICKLY, and it wasn't long before Mrs. Thompson confronted Aminata. Her face was twisted in a mask of rage. "You vile creature!" she screamed. "How dare you bring this disgrace into my home?"

Mr. Thompson, on the other hand, was a mix of confusion and denial. He avoided Aminata's eyes, unable to reconcile his lust with the growing life inside her. He muttered to himself, debating whether to acknowledge the child or dismiss it as nothing more than a mistake.

Mrs. Thompson's decision was swift and ruthless. "Get out of my house," she hissed. "You belong in the fields with the rest of the animals."

Aminata was sent back to the fields, her once slight frame now carrying the weight of her pregnancy and the burden of her fate. The sun beat down mercilessly as she worked, her body straining under the added load.

Each day in the fields was an ordeal. The physical toll of pregnancy, combined with the back-breaking labor, was nearly unbearable. Her legs ached, her back throbbed, and her feet were swollen and sore. Yet, she pushed on, driven by an indomitable will to survive.

The overseers showed no mercy. They barked orders and wielded their whips, indifferent to her condition. Each lash felt like fire on her skin, a constant reminder of her status and her suffering.

The other slaves watched with sympathy and sorrow. They offered what little comfort they could, sharing their food and providing words of encouragement. Mama June, ever the maternal figure, took special care to look after Aminata.

"Drink dis, child," she said one evening, handing Aminata a cup of herbal tea. "It'll help wit' de sickness."

Aminata took the cup, her hands trembling. "Thank you, Mama June," she whispered, grateful for the small kindness.

· · · ·

THE MONTHS DRAGGED on, each day a test of her resilience. The baby grew inside her, a mix of hope and dread. She wondered what kind of life awaited her child, born into a world of bondage and brutality.

Her body bore the scars of her struggle. The lashes from the whip, the bruises from the hard labor, and the constant ache in her muscles were daily reminders of her plight. Yet, she endured, fueled by a fierce determination to survive for the sake of her unborn child.

Amid the hardship, whispers of rebellion floated through the fields. Some slaves spoke of escaping, of finding freedom beyond the confines of the plantation. Others told stories of uprisings, where slaves had risen against their masters.

"We ain't meant to live like dis," Isaac said one night, his voice a low growl. "One day, we gon' rise up. We gon' fight for our freedom."

Aminata listened, her heart stirred by their words. She clung to the hope of a better future, a life where her child could grow up free and unchained.

One particularly grueling day, Aminata collapsed in the field. The pain in her belly was sharp and unrelenting, and she knew the time was near. The overseers dragged her to the makeshift infirmary, where Mama June and a few other slaves helped her through the labor.

The night was long and filled with agony. Aminata screamed and cried, her body racked with pain. But she fought on, her mind focused on the life she was bringing into the world.

As dawn broke, Aminata gave birth to a baby boy. He was small and frail, but he cried with a strength that filled her heart with hope. She held him close, tears streaming down her face.

"He's beautiful," Mama June said, smiling despite the tears in her own eyes.

Aminata looked at her son, a mix of love and fear in her heart. She knew the challenges that lay ahead, but she vowed to protect him with every ounce of strength she had.

Life on the plantation continued, but now Aminata had a new purpose. She worked tirelessly, her son a constant source of strength and motivation. She faced the daily hardships with renewed determination, knowing that she was fighting not just for herself, but for her child's future.

Mr. Thompson's attitude remained conflicted. He avoided Aminata and her son, unable to face the reality of his actions. Mrs. Thompson's hatred, however, burned even brighter. She took every opportunity to humiliate and punish Aminata, her jealousy and spite knowing no bounds.

One day, as Aminata was working in the field with her baby strapped to her back, Mrs. Thompson approached with a cruel smile. "Your bastard child will never know a day of peace," she sneered. "I will make sure of that."

Aminata's blood boiled, but she kept her head down, refusing to give Mrs. Thompson the satisfaction of seeing her anger.

Despite the cruelty and hardship, Aminata found moments of joy and solace. The other slaves became her family, their shared struggles forging bonds of unbreakable strength. They sang songs in the fields, their voices a testament to their resilience and hope.

One evening, as the sun set over the horizon, the slaves gathered around a fire. Isaac began to sing, his deep voice resonating through the night.

• • • •

"WALK TOGETHER, CHILDREN, Don't you get weary,
Walk together, children, Don't you get weary,
Oh, talk together, children, Don't you get weary,
There's a great camp meeting in the Promised Land."

The others joined in, their voices rising in a powerful chorus. Aminata held her son close, her heart lifted by the song. She knew that no matter the hardships, they would endure. They would find a way to survive, and one day, they would find their freedom.

The months turned into years, and Aminata's son grew strong under her watchful care. She taught him the values of resilience and hope, instilling in him the belief that they would one day be free.

The whispers of rebellion grew louder, the seeds of resistance taking root. Aminata knew that their journey was far from over, but she was ready to face whatever lay ahead with courage and determination. She would honor her mother's legacy by never giving up, by fighting for a future where her son could grow up free and unchained.

As she looked at her son, Aminata saw the promise of a better tomorrow. She knew that the road ahead would be difficult, but she was ready to fight with every ounce of strength she had. For her son, for her fellow slaves, and for the hope of a future filled with freedom and justice, Aminata vowed to never give up.

The journey was far from over, but Aminata's spirit burned bright, a beacon of hope in a world filled with darkness. She knew that one day, they would find their freedom, and she would fight with every ounce of strength she had to achieve it. Would she? The story continues...

ABOUT THE AUTHOR

Eddie Inyangala is a multifaceted creative force, excelling as a psychologist, linguist, scholar, poet, writer, editor, artist, and DJ. With a rich background that weaves together the understanding of the human mind and the beauty of language, Eddie brings a unique perspective to storytelling. His work captures the depth of human emotions and experiences, reflecting his diverse talents and profound insights. Through his writing, Eddie continues to explore and illuminate the complexities of African life, culture, and identity.

Michael R.: "Every book by Eddie Inyangala is a new adventure. His ability to blend historical context with rich character development is incredible. I highly recommend his works to anyone who loves thought-provoking literature."

Linda S.: "Eddie Inyangala's novels are a testament to his immense talent. His unique perspective and engaging writing style make him one of my favorite authors. I can't wait to see what he writes next!"

Don't miss out!

Visit the website below and you can sign up to receive emails whenever EDDIE INYANGALA publishes a new book. There's no charge and no obligation.

https://books2read.com/r/B-A-ATHRB-ZDCPD

BOOKS 2 READ

Connecting independent readers to independent writers.

About the Author

Michael R.: "Every book by Eddie Inyangala is a new adventure. His ability to blend historical context with rich character development is incredible. I highly recommend his works to anyone who loves thought-provoking literature."

Linda S.: "Eddie Inyangala's novels are a testament to his immense talent. His unique perspective and engaging writing style make him one of my favorite authors. I can't wait to see what he writes next!"